EAST

Praise for Kirk Kjeldsen's *East*

East's cli-fi futurescape is both sobering and gripping . . .
If hope is not the point of the novel, its unflinching
consideration of what might be ahead for human beings is.
– *Foreword Reviews*

Fascinating, austere, and deeply humane. Kjeldsen's *East* is
the story of an undocumented American immigrant in a
near-future China, which is to say it's our world turned on
its head, which is really to say: It's our world.
– Aaron Thier, author of *Mr. Eternity*
and *The World Is a Narrow Bridge*

What you can reliably expect from Kjeldsen is a keen
imagination and fine writing . . . In *East*, he spins a
mesmerizing story -- fantastic, yes, but so clearly rooted in
the most palpable anxieties that characterize today's
America that it feels eerily, chillingly prescient.
– *New Jersey Star-Ledger*

East is a pitch-dark, beautifully written coming-of-age
story that turns the American Dream trope inside out, as
young Job flees the ravaged wastelands of the Pacific
Coast and undergoes a dizzying, desperate journey to find
salvation in China. The narrative is taut and gripping, the
characters vivid and real, and the story breathtaking.
– Jennie Melamed, author of *Gather the Daughters*

Strong tale of a bleak future seen through the eyes of one
determined individual . . . Kjeldsen does an excellent job
of building Job's damaged world, drawing vivid scenes . . .
the fast-paced plot will keep readers turning pages.
– *Kirkus Reviews*

East provides a powerful, hard-boiled narrative about a
world where abundance is a fairy tale and migrants have
to endure horror in order to work, travel, and find their

loved ones. It is a dystopian *future* only because it is about Americans migrating to distant lands, but it speaks about us, today, since this is precisely the present that migrants face in the United States. Beyond nationalities, it is about the human determination to never stand still.

– Yuri Herrera, author of *Signs Preceding the End of the World* and *Kingdom Cons*

Praise for Kirk Kjeldsen's *The Depths*

A sensational book—an absolute fever blister of a thriller that manages also to be a fine, nearly heartbreaking character study. I'll be recommending it all year.

– Timothy Hallinan, author of the Poke Rafferty and Junior Bender novels

Kjeldsen's plot pulses with electricity, his prose offers rich descriptions of the tropical environment, and his characters brim with life. A thriller with striking originality and an uncommon setting, *The Depths* takes readers to the heights of nerve-jangling suspense.

– *Richmond Times-Dispatch*

A gut punch of a thriller, wickedly paced, and beautifully rendered.

– Peter Swanson, author of *Her Every Fear* and *The Kind Worth Killing*

Kjeldsen's short novel moves at a blistering pace, putting Marah through one ordeal after another . . . This tense, haunting tale gives readers front-row seats to the protagonist's torment.

– *Kirkus Reviews*

Note to literary thriller fans: If you haven't discovered Kirk Kjeldsen, it's time. Unlike some overwritten, hyped-up, device-laden novels in the genre, Kjeldsen's novels are thoughtfully plotted, spare in the telling, and beautifully written. *The Depths* is not merely a compelling thriller with unexpected turns, but a study of a psychologically tormented woman who must plumb her own depths to save herself and her husband . . . His meticulous attention to language makes for a story that is as pictorial as it is riveting.

– New Jersey Star-Ledger

The Depths is a wonderful novel: lyrical, yet still relentless and utterly engrossing. Few writers have explored the ragged fault line where western sensibilities struggle with the enigmas of Asia, and absolutely no one has done it better than this.

– Jake Needham, author of the Jack Shepherd and Inspector Samuel Tay novels

With strong prose and stunning imagery, *The Depths* takes the thriller genre to the next level . . . a pleasurable read, immensely satisfying in its suspense.

– IndieReader

The Depths is everything you look for in a literary thriller: transporting, suspenseful, beautifully written, and above all soaked in every type and shade of dread you can possibly imagine.

– Estep Nagy, author of We Shall Not All Sleep

Praise for Kirk Kjeldsen's *Land of Hidden Fires*

Kjeldsen tells a small-scale tale about Norwegian resistance to the Nazis in this work that should appeal to historical thriller fans . . . His descriptive prose does a fine job of conveying the breathtaking scenery of the wintry Norwegian mountains.

– Publishers Weekly

Land of Hidden Fires is a compelling testament to the dangers, and necessity, of resistance. Kjeldsen writes about the quiet horrors of life in wartime with clear-eyed humanity and grace.

> – Colin Winnette, author of *Haints Stay* and
> *The Job of the Wasp*

Creating tension is just one of Kjeldsen's talents. Another is utterly capturing the mindset of a sheltered teenage girl who is falling in love with her rescued (and indifferent) pilot, imagining herself going to America with him. And third, but far from last, is Kjeldsen's writing. He has masterfully set a story, fraught throughout with danger, against an icy, white, virtually silent tableau—a story that will stay with you long after you've finished it.

> – *New Jersey Star-Ledger*

A fine wartime tale of survival and resistance, told with clean, compelling prose. The tough and resourceful Kari will linger in your memory, and the evocative setting will leave you shivering beneath the sheets.

> – Dan Fesperman, author of *The Letter Writer*
> and *Safe Houses*

Kirk Kjeldsen's nonfiction turned novel is a fitting memorial to heroes whose lights shine in dark times . . . The novel is full of suspense and drama, and the author succeeds in casting light on a very dark period of Norway's history.

> – *The Norwegian American*

As much a love letter to his family's homeland as it is a thrilling adventure of World War II, Kirk Kjeldsen's *Land of Hidden Fires* shows that underneath Norway's snow and ice lies a burning heart.

> – Alan Gratz, author of *Prisoner B-3087*

Also by Kirk Kjeldsen

TOMORROW CITY
LAND OF HIDDEN FIRES
THE DEPTHS

EAST

A novel
Kirk Kjeldsen

Grenzland Press

East
By Kirk Kjeldsen
Published by Grenzland Press
Copyright © 2019 Kirk Kjeldsen
ISBN: 978-0-9984657-5-3
eBook ISBN: 978-0-9984657-6-0

www.grenzlandpress.com

Cover design: Adly Elewa
Editors: Luke Gerwe, Anne McPeak
Proofreader: Ryan Quinn
Author photograph: SoMi Fotographie

for Lauren,
again

"We're not only a nation of immigrants, but we are in some part a nation of emigrants, which often gets neglected."

—Samuel P. Huntington

"Hard is the journey,
Hard is the journey,
So many turnings,
And now where am I?"

—Li Po

It didn't happen overnight, but it happened. It must have happened so slow that no one noticed, no one did a thing to try and stop it. Or maybe they did, but it was just too big to stop, like the floodwaters the Willamette brought every now and then. My grandfather used to talk about the old days when I was little, the days before the SEZs and the maquilas, when it was all still a united country and not a bunch of squabbling little ones. When the Cascades weren't gutted and the earth wasn't all churned up and fracked. But I never believed him. And why should I have? I always thought he was just a crazy old man pining for something that never was. Turns out maybe he wasn't so crazy after all.

One day when I was eight or nine, I found an old magazine that had pictures in it. I was down by the river checking the frog traps. It came floating along in the slurry, bobbing and torn up, the cover half-gone. After I fished it out with my push pole, I opened it. The pages were all stuck together, and most of the images had bled away, but in the few that weren't, people were laughing and having fun. They all had bright white teeth in perfect little rows, and they all had thick and shiny hair. And their skin was perfect. Every single one of them. No one had cholera. No one had TB or cancer. No one was yellow or splotchy or jaundiced. They were all sitting out by pools of clean water and playing out on wide open fields or sitting inside by warm fires. A few of the pictures showed food, too, and showed the people eating, and the things they were eating were almost cartoonish. Loaves of bread like pillows. Fruits every color of the rainbow. Big cuts of meat, all shiny and pink and dripping with juice. There were no flies, no maggots, no rot. If it hadn't been for Grandpa's stories, I would've thought the pictures weren't real. I brought them home and showed them to Eli, but he said they weren't worth looking at and that you couldn't bring back the past and that it was better to just move on. But I kept one of them, a big one that had hardly any writing on it at all. It showed a group of people inside a large house that had books on shelves and bright lights and fancy furniture. There was a man and a woman and two children, a boy and a girl. They looked like a family. There was a dog, too. It was the fattest dog I'd ever seen—you couldn't even see its ribs. And it was just lying there near their table, sleeping. The man was sitting at the head of the table and had a glass of something in front of him with cubes of ice floating in it, and he was smiling. The boy was smiling, too. They were all watching the little girl, who was standing on her chair, waving a sparkly wand. She was all dressed up with fake

16

shiny wings, and she had ribbons in her hair. The woman was pouring glasses of milk for the children, and in the middle of the table there was a tray of some steaming food that must've been cheesy spaghetti bake as there was a container in the lower right-hand corner of the picture that had those words on it. And at the bottom of the picture, it read, "Every family dinner is a great story waiting to happen." For years I carried that picture around. Folded it up tight and kept it inside Grandpa's worn-out leather wallet. I carried it around long after it had started to come apart and became two pieces and then four and then eight. Every night I'd put the pieces back together like they were pieces of a puzzle, and I'd stare at them before I went to sleep. I'd dream that our family would someday be like the family in that picture, and that the parents I could not remember would come back and join us, and that we'd all be seated around a great table, bathed in a warm light and excited for what was to come.

I

Job woke while it was still dark and rose from his nest of moldy blankets, his ghost-pale fourteen-year-old body as knotty and gnarled as a gingko root. He pulled on his mismatched boots as quietly as he could; the one was an old, oil-tanned jodhpur he'd found on a drowned miner and was as broken in and soft as an animal pelt, and it made no sound as he stepped into it. The other was a lace-up work boot that was a size too big and was fastened together with baling wire and wouldn't go on without a struggle. As he tried to shove his foot into it, the rusty lattice holding it together creaked just enough to make his older brother Eli stir on the other side of the room.

Job froze and looked to where the jaundiced teen lay half-asleep on a tarp-covered pile of bagged leaves and soggy rolls of fiberglass insulation. Eli's brow was clenched tight and slicked with sweat, and his pale and cancer-splotched arms were wrapped around a roll of insulation like the wings of some wrecked bird trying to protect its young. Job stood there for a long moment, watching his brother and wondering what dark and buried thoughts were furrowing his brow. After Eli finally fell back into a fitful sleep, Job began to creep his way toward the other room.

On the other side of the shack, he found a plastic jug half-full of rainwater and took a long swig. Despite boiling, the water was still milky and tasted like copper, but it was better than the river water he was forced to drink during droughts. After capping the jug, he pulled on the work boot and a poncho he'd fashioned from another old tarp. Then he picked up his quiver and bow, unlocked the rusty bicycle chain binding the door, and went outside into the wet dawn.

He quietly made his way through the village. The run-down shacks and trailers were all dark, and there was no one outside. As he approached the forest, he passed the halved oil tank they used to collect rainwater; greasy rainbows shimmered on the surface of the water pooling in the tank and contorted or broke apart as the breeze changed directions. Overhead, the sky was the color of tarnished gunmetal, and the air was clear as there'd been a rain sometime during the night, but it still smelled like sulfur and burned hair. Underneath a derelict school bus, a pair of mangy cats fought over an animal fetus, and in the distance, a thin column of smoke rose and dissipated in the wind.

Once he reached the forest, Job stuck to the winding trail that ran alongside the Willamette. He found a tiny pair of speckled brown eggs in an abandoned nest and carefully wrapped them in an oil-stained rag before putting them away. Farther on, he stopped to cut a two-foot shoot off a hickory with his penny knife. He slid the hickory shoot into his quiver and broke off from the trail when he found a set of beaver tracks heading away from the water and into the forest. It'd been some time since he'd seen such tracks, but he knew with certainty what they were by the way the tail dragged over them and softened their sharp outlines. The thought of fresh beaver meat made his stomach growl, and he drew and nocked an arrow as he followed the trail. A few hundred yards into the forest, though, the tracks abruptly switchbacked toward the river and then stopped altogether, leaving no trace of where the animal had gone or what had happened to it other than a few leaves spotted with black blood.

He pushed deeper into the forest as the morning went on; aside from the intermittent trail of a sage grouse, and a drowned pygmy rabbit he found in a collapsed burrow, his searches yielded nothing. When he got to Yachats Ridge, Job turned around and began to head home. Before he got far, though, he noticed a faint scent on the breeze; it was musky and earthy yet sickly sweet, like butter gone bad.

Job soon heard a branch snap somewhere in the forest ahead of him. He got low to the ground and crept forward, changing his direction slightly enough so he could approach whatever it was from the flank. As he saw a dark shape flash through the tree line, he raised his bow and nocked an arrow and drew back the bowstring. Then he spotted his wan brother emerging from the underbrush.

"Sweet Jesus," said Eli. "What are you doing?"

"What's it look like I'm doing?" said Job, letting the bowstring go slack.

"How'd you find me?"

"Wasn't hard, what with all the racket you were making."

Eli shook with a fit of coughing, speckling the back of his hand with blood-tinged mucus. Job shoved the arrow back into his quiver before carefully reaching into his pocket and pulling out the tiny eggs.

"You hungry?" he asked.

"Where'd you find those?"

"There was a nest just a ways back. Hell, you practically stepped on it."

Eli shook his head and spat in the dirt.

"Well," said Job. "You want one or not?"

Eli took one of the eggs from Job and cracked it open above his mouth. Job did the same with the other egg.

When they finished sucking the stringy albumen from the gritty shells, they spit them onto the ground. Then they descended the ridge and made their way back into the valley.

They silently followed two sets of tracks for the better part of the morning. The first set had belonged to a canine, but some other predator had gotten to it before they had and had left nothing but the violent shorthand of a struggle and a messy pile of entrail-matted bones. The second set of tracks they came upon belonged to a squirrel; judging by its scat, it couldn't have been older than a fledgling and wouldn't have made a meal for just one of them. They followed the trail to its end at an old and gnarled myrtle tree where they found no sign of where the squirrel had gone, but they did find a number of cracked and empty bay nut hulls. Realizing the squirrel had either been snatched up by a hawk or had jumped to another tree, Job shinnied up the myrtle and plucked the remainder of the bay nuts off the tree's spindly branches as Eli waited down below, gathering the ones that eluded Job's grasp.

After filling their pockets, they continued through the valley before beginning to circle back toward the Willamette. At midday, the sun was hardly visible through the pollution, as if a palely colored iris behind a thick cataract. Eli grew winded and wanted to give up and return home, but Job convinced him to continue on, and

before long, they noticed some broken branches at the
edge of a clearing. When they approached the clearing
edge, they found an oddly spaced set of tracks cutting
through a dry riverbed, and they knelt down and studied
them like two young monks poring over an ancient
manuscript.

"What do you make of these?" asked Eli.

"They're deer."

"Yeah, I know they're deer."

"Then why'd you ask?"

"I meant what's with the spacing?" said Eli. "I can't
tell if there's one or two of them or if they're walking or
running or what."

"Only one way to find out."

They followed the tracks along the riverbed and then
up a ridge and along a shelf of uneven rock. The tracks
grew closer together for stretches but continued to be
irregularly spaced like some rambling and incoherent
message tapped out in Morse code. The faint sun moved
behind its thick curtain of smog from their right side to
their left as they traversed the other side of the ridge and
headed down into another valley. Soon the tracks began to
change direction and darted back and forth as if the
animal had panicked. Job and Eli left the trail when they
reached the floodplain, knowing there was a river ahead
and that the animal would be stopping there whether it
wanted to or not.

They moved silently and quickly through the low hills. After following a dry creek bed, they reached the river just before the animal arrived. Job was the first to see the scrawny doe when it emerged from the forest, walk-hopping on its three legs.

"Well," he said in a low voice. "That answers that."

Eli said nothing and watched as the doe wheeled up to and away from the water's edge, uncertain of its next move. The animal's ribs stood out on its side like the bars of a xylophone, and slobber hung from its lips in gluey strings.

"You gonna shoot it or what?" asked Job.

Eli hesitated. After a moment, Job shook his head and raised his bow. He nocked an arrow, drew back the bowstring, and took aim. The animal lifted its tired head and looked in their direction, but before their gazes met, Job let his arrow fly. The arrow punched through the animal's mangy hide just below its right shoulder, and the animal pitched forward whining and plowed nose first into the dirt.

Job lowered the bow and stepped forward to approach the fallen animal, but before he could get there, a man with a duct-taped rifle slung over his shoulder emerged from the forest upstream. The man reached the doe first and picked up the dead animal by its scruff, and Job rushed toward the man in a rage.

"What the hell are you doing?" he said. "That's ours."

"Bullshit," said the man, spitting the words through a ragged fence of rotten teeth. "I shot him first. Look here."

The man lifted the doe to show them. Its haunches were peppered with rat shot and matted with drips of coagulating blood.

"That's nothing," said Job.

"The hell it's nothing."

"Give it back."

Job reached for the doe, but the man pulled it away. Eli moved forward and grabbed Job by the shoulder.

"Let's go," he said.

"We're not going," said Job. "That's our deer."

Job pulled away from Eli and lunged again for the carcass, and again the man snatched it away.

"You're a feisty little one, aren't you—"

Before the man could finish, Job kicked him in the groin. The man dropped the doe and fell wheezing to his knees.

"Motherfucker—"

Job picked up the carcass, and the man struggled to his feet, swinging the rifle off his shoulder and aiming it at Job. Eli fumbled forth an arrow and drew back his bowstring, pointing the arrow at the man.

"Careful there, mister," said Eli, the arrow wobbling in his trembling fingers.

"What are you gonna do, shoot me?" said the man.

"If I have to."

"You don't have the sack."

25

Before Eli could reply, a voice bellowed from the forest behind them.

"What in the shit?"

Job and Eli turned to see a stocky woman approaching, armed with a rusty rifle. Her scalp was a checkerboard of stringy black hair and raw red and white skin, the byproduct of alopecia or cancer or some hybrid of the two.

"These little bastards are trying to take our deer," said the man.

The woman raised her rifle and pointed it at Eli.

"I'd lower that if I was you, boy," she said.

"Tell your man to lower his first," said Eli.

The man turned and aimed his rifle at Job.

"Give me the deer, you little prick," he said.

"No way," said Job.

"You want to die? Give me the fucking deer."

Job said nothing and stood his ground, hugging the doe to his chest and looking like a child holding a sullied rag doll.

"You heard him," said the woman. "Now give it over."

They stood there for a long moment, locked in a standoff. Eli looked toward Job, pleading with his eyes, but Job refused his glance.

"I'm gonna count to three," said the man. "Then I'm gonna shoot."

Job didn't move. The man's eyes narrowed.

"One," he said.

"Give him the deer," said Eli.

Job shook his head and continued to stare down the man.

"Two," said the man, his eyes flashing with rage.

"Do what he says," said the woman.

Job continued to stand firm. After a moment, the man shoved in the rifle's bolt action and cocked a shell into the chamber, but before he could pull the trigger, Job dropped the carcass at the man's feet.

"Smart boy," said the man.

The man slung the rifle over his shoulder and picked up the animal, and the woman backed up toward the forest from where she'd come, keeping her rifle pointed at them.

"Better hope you don't run into us again," said the woman. "We might not be so friendly next time."

Job and Eli watched the man and the woman disappear back into the woods. As soon as they were gone, Eli lowered the bow and let the bowstring go slack. His face was as pale as ash, and his clothes were soaked with sweat.

"We shouldn't have given it to them," said Job.

"What else were we gonna do? Shoot 'em?"

"That was our deer."

Eli responded in a strained voice.

"Come on," he said. "Let's go home."

Eli turned and stumbled off, and Job slung his bow over his shoulder and followed his brother. Before they'd gotten far, Eli broke into a fit of coughing. Then he fell to one knee before pitching forward and face first into the dirt.

"You all right?" asked Job.

Eli didn't respond. Job rushed over and knelt next to his brother. He shook Eli's shoulder, but Eli didn't respond. With some effort, he turned him onto his back; Eli's eyes rolled white in their sockets, and a wet stain began to spread at the crotch of his pants.

"Eli?"

Job shook his brother again, but Eli still didn't respond. Job lowered his ear to Eli's chest and listened for a heartbeat, but it was as still as the bottom of a lake.

Then he heard a faint rustling murmur in Eli's lungs, like some dried leaves fluttering across a forest floor.

Job fashioned a makeshift stretcher out of branches, using their bowstrings to fasten it together. He tied Eli to the stretcher and then dragged it through the forest, taking a winding route to avoid the inclines. By the time he reached the outskirts of their village, it was already past midnight. Sharp stabbing pains shot up his back from the base of his spine all the way to his neck.

When he finally reached their shack, Job carried his brother through the low door and into their shelter. He deposited his brother onto the tarp-covered pile of leaves and insulation rolls. Then he lit the blackened wick of their colza lamp. The greasy yellow light it quickly bore threw long flickering shadows against the walls.

Job lit a fire, then got down a battered steel pot from their cupboard. He emptied the contents of his pockets into the pot and collected the bay nuts from Eli's pockets as well, using his penny knife to split them open and cut the hard seeds from their fatty flesh. The flesh was too unripe to eat, so he saved the halved husks to dry them out in the sun. Once the nuts were shelled, he set them by the fire for roasting. He chucked a few more logs onto the fire and then took off his boots and clothes and set them by the fire to dry. Then he lay down near his brother and closed his eyes. Before long he slept, and when he slept he had no dreams, and when he woke in the predawn morning the house smelled like burned chocolate and wet fur, and the fire had died down and it was cold again.

Job gathered the roasted bay nuts and put them into a plastic bag. After he was finished, he tossed a few more logs onto the fire, then pulled his dried clothes back on and left the shelter. He brought the nuts to a wide shack at the other end of the village. There was no light inside, so he waited until a light finally appeared an hour later, and as soon as it did he knocked on the door of the shack with his balled fist. No one came, so he knocked again and again until he could finally hear a heavy pair of feet shuffling across the floor inside. A moment later, the door unlocked and opened to reveal Old Lady Simons. She clutched a sawed-off shotgun in her hard, knobby hands, and her swollen bosom was barely contained by the ratty nightgown she wore.

"Good God, child, what time is it?" she said, lowering her shotgun when she recognized him.

"I saw your candle."

"Hell, I just lit it but two seconds ago."

"Well, are you open or not?"

She shook her head, turned, and walked off, but she left the door open. Job took that as an invitation, and he followed her inside.

"What in the hell's so important you're here at the crack of dawn?" she asked.

Job dropped the bag of roasted bay nuts onto the store's makeshift counter.

"How much will you give me for these?" he asked.

The old woman pointed to a shelf full of canned goods, batteries, and other sundries.

"I got plenty of nuts—"

He interrupted her.

"You don't have these," he said. "They're fresh. Not like them canned nuts you get from the city."

"People don't want that stuff."

"I'll give them to you for a tin of sardines."

"Son—"

"Will you give me something or not?"

She hesitated.

"Fine," said Job. "You won't be getting my business no more."

Before she could reply, Job grabbed the bag of nuts and left. Outside, the sky was streaked with pale dabs of yellow and gray, and life was returning to the village. Tired-looking women boiled water and cooked lupin beans or rats or whatever else they could find over small fires, trying to scratch together their meals. An old man worked on a disassembled motorcycle engine, and a girl with Down syndrome wearing a puffy jacket rocked and sang to herself. There were no young men anywhere, and the few young women that there were were taking care of the elderly and the very young.

When Job returned to their shelter, he found the fire dying again. After he chucked a few more logs onto it from their dwindling supply, his brother spoke from the other side of the room; his voice was parched and thin, and it sounded like wind from a dust storm.

"Who's there?" he said.

"It's just me," said Job.

Eli broke into a fit of coughing. Job grabbed the jug of water and brought it over to him. Eli looked like a ghost, spectral and half-hidden by the flickering shadows. His brow was hot to the touch, and it was rimed with salt.

"Drink this," said Job.

He raised the jug to his brother's lips, and Eli took a pull and choked on it.

"Not so fast," said Job.

After he swallowed some water, Eli glanced up. His gaze was vacant and far off, as if he was looking through Job and toward some unseen object in the distance. After a long moment, he spoke.

"You remember them stories Grandpa used to tell us?" he said. "'Bout the seven-horned lamb and the wormwood star and the world to come?"

Job said nothing.

"'Behold, the tabernacle of God is with men, and he will dwell with them . . .'"

"Easy."

"'God shall wipe away all tears from their eyes, and there shall be no more death, neither sorrow, nor crying, neither shall there be any more pain, for the former things are passed away . . .'"

His voice trailed off, and he glanced around as if he'd forgotten where he was.

"How did it go then?" he said, and then remembering, he continued: "'Behold, I make all things new . . . I am the Alpha and Omega. The beginning and the end . . .'"

"Go on," said Job, offering Eli the bag of roasted bay nuts. "Eat some of these."

"They're not gonna help."

"Sure, they are."

"I'm dying."

"No, you're not."

"Yeah, I am. I can feel it. It's like a fire going out or something."

Eli broke into another fit of coughing.

"You're gonna be fine," said Job.

"I need to tell you something," said Eli, struggling to sit up.

"You need to eat—"

Eli interrupted him.

"It's about Ma," he said.

Job offered the jug to his brother again.

"Go on," he said. "Drink some more."

"She didn't die," said Eli.

"Hogwash."

"I'm serious," said Eli. "She ran off. Went to China after Pa left."

"What for?"

"For work, what else? We didn't have shit."

Job considered it for a moment before shaking his head.

"You're lying," he said.

"No, I'm not," said Eli. "She said she was gonna send for us, too. Even sent a letter once, when we were still living by town."

Job shook his head again but said nothing, wondering if it was actually true.

"I got it in a box somewhere," said Eli.

"Why didn't you tell me?" said Job, his voice suddenly strained.

"What was I supposed to say?" said Eli. "That she abandoned us? Christ, you were only three or four."

"You still should've told me."

"I thought it would've been easier for you if you thought she was dead."

"How is that easier?"

Eli broke into another fit of coughing. Then it subsided, and they sat there in silence for a long moment, watching the flames flicker and diminish.

After a while, Eli spoke again.

"You should try to find her," he said.

"I'm not going to China."

"You got no reason to stay here."

"Sure, I do. I got you."

"Not for long."

"Quit talking like that."

"You can have a better life there."

"Just drop it, all right?" said Job. "You just need some meat in you, that's all. You get some meat in you and you'll be strong again, you'll see."

Before Eli could reply, Job stood and went for his bow.

"Wait," said Eli.

Ignoring him, Job approached the door.

"I'll be back before sundown," he said. "Just try and rest, okay? I'll ask Dell Eckie to look in on you."

Eli opened his mouth to reply, but before he could, Job hurried out the door.

He wandered the forest. In the early afternoon, he followed a feral cat into the valley and lost its tracks at a creek and then found them again downstream on the other side of the creek and followed them across the land. A cold wind came down from the mountains to the north and west and brought with it the first signs of autumn; the few remaining leaves of the trees were beginning to turn, and Job could smell their musty perfume on the dry breeze.

He came to a desiccated riverbed and followed the tracks across the cracked and curling mud. As the river bent westward, he shielded his eyes from the blood-red sun as it sank shimmering toward the barren mountains. When he finally caught up with the animal, he drew and nocked an arrow, but when he saw the animal's wasted body, he hesitated. Its raw open nose and mouth were slicked with blood and pus, and its teeth poked out through its eroded grin. As it breathed in and out in short ragged breaths, it kept sneezing and shaking its head. The animal seemed to be pleading to him somehow and he considered putting it out of its misery, but he paused, wondering if he was really capable of making such a decision, and who or what might be worthy of arbitrating such a thing.

Before he could make up his mind, the animal turned and limped off downriver, sneezing as it went. Job let the bowstring go slack and then changed direction and headed off into the forest. He followed a meandering trail for a while and then went up a ridge and followed the trail along the crest and then down toward a pass on the other side. When he reached the pass, he saw a blue-black shadow flatten against the darkening sky before him and then watched as a peregrine folded back its tail and its wings and slashed down toward the earth like a falling sickle and snatched up a vole outside its crumbling burrow. As the peregrine opened its wings and rose back up grasping its prey, Job nocked and loosed an arrow. Then he watched it sail whistling through the breeze until there was a puff of feather, and the creature froze for the briefest of moments and then twisted and tumbled awkwardly back to the earth with the arrow locked in its breast.

He went forward to look for the peregrine and found it crumpled near a stand of cottonwood trees. The vole was ripped to tatters in the bird's still-clenched, yolk-yellow claws. He pulled the arrow from the peregrine and wiped it across his pants, then he looked at the carcass: the bird's remains bore little resemblance to the creature that had carved its way through the air only moments before. All the life was gone from its inky eyes, and in the dying light its black crown contrasted sharply with its cream-colored throat and made it look like a puppet that had been cast aside by a child.

He carefully wrapped the peregrine in a piece of burlap and put it into his sling. Then he turned and headed back for the village. By the time he got there, it was nearly dark again. Some of the villagers were outside doing the last of their daily tasks or were gathering firewood for the coming night.

Job called for his brother when he entered their shack through the low door, but there was no reply. He went into the other room, immediately noticing that the fire had gone out. Then he spotted Eli on his back, stone still and staring blankly at the ceiling.

He didn't need to check for a pulse to know that his brother was dead.

The chalky skies over the valley grew heavy with clouds, and a cool breeze came shearing down from the mountains. The world grew quiet for a while, and the dead leaves whispered in the trees and the dragonflies came and left and then the clouds finally opened. It rained, and it rained hard and fast and heavy, and when the winds came, the rain slashed down diagonally and even sideways at times and washed away the blanket of soot and grime that covered the village. The rain drummed down onto the rooftops, and it pounded against the windows and walls, and it seeped in through cracks and holes and whatever other pregnable areas it could find. It made the earth soft and it shaped runnels and streams where none had been, and these waters found courses reckoned by gravity and flowed downhill carrying the flotsam of the village along with them and cut shallow grooves into the mud and exposed buried rocks and garbage and bones.

For two days and two nights, Job sat by the body of his brother. It was as if he'd been in the middle of a journey through some darkened jungle, and his map had suddenly been wiped clean of all its lines and symbols and had become a blank parchment. He felt empty and as if he no longer knew where he was nor where he was going, and he had no polestar or compass to help him find his way.

On the third night, he finally began to think clearly again, and as he lay by the fire, he tried to come up with a reason not to search for his mother. He wondered if things would be any different if he moved upriver, or if he'd have luck going to the mines or the maquilas down south. He knew it wasn't any different up or downriver, though, and he knew the mines and maquilas paid little, and he'd heard far too many stories about people getting buried in explosions or getting cancer from all the solvents and silica they churned out. When he finally fell asleep, Job dreamed of the forest. In the dream, he was near a creek in a valley where they used to go looking for crawfish when there were still crawfish to be found, making his way toward a section of the Willamette that had long since been turned into lake by a dam downriver. He was alone, but he did not feel alone somehow, as if perhaps his brother or his grandfather or some benevolent spirit accompanied him. He had his bow over his shoulder and a quiver full of arrows on his back, and he was following a set of rabbit tracks heading toward the lake. When he reached the lake, though, he found it dry.

Job looked out at the vast lake bed and saw scores of old farmhouses. He walked out and approached one of them, the dried lake floor crumbling to dust beneath his feet. When he got to the farmhouse, he knocked at the door, but no one answered. Then he checked the door and found it unlocked, so he went inside. No one was there, but it wasn't abandoned; the rooms were furnished and appeared lived in. A bowl of fresh fruit stood on a table, and some dirty plates filled the kitchen sink.

Before long, Job left the empty farmhouse and approached another. Again, he knocked at the door, but again, no one answered. He went inside and saw that it was also furnished and lived in, though no one was there. A mug of coffee cooled on a table, and some drying laundry hung outside.

He left and went into another house, and he found it also lived in but empty. As he looked through its kitchen, he began to hear a low rolling sound building in the distance. It sounded like far-off thunder at first, but it didn't stop or go away and kept growing in volume. Job went over to one of the windows and looked outside, but he saw nothing. Then he went to the back of the house and looked through a screen door, and he saw a tidal wave of black water slowly surging toward him. It grew and rose as it approached and chewed up houses and trees and everything else in its path, and the rolling sound became louder and louder and it soon blocked out the sun and his screams and everything else. Then he woke in his pile of blankets, gasping for air.

As Job glanced around the shack getting his bearings, he saw his brother's body across from him, stiff with rigor mortis. He saw their barren cupboards, and then he saw the dying fire, where the last few coals flared with bright and jagged red crazing. He got up, went over to the cupboard, and drank some water; his tongue was leather, and he had a dull headache that throbbed behind his eyes. Once he finished drinking, he looked through the slat in the door. Outside, the sun wasn't quite up yet, but it was beginning to climb into the sky at the edge of the horizon.

He got a small spade and went out toward the tree line beyond their shelter. There, he approached the clearing where his grandfather was buried in a grave marked by a large, flat stone. He plunged the spade into the earth next to his grandfather's grave and began digging. He kept digging even after the hole seemed more than deep enough and he didn't stop until the spade finally bit sparking into a large stone.

He went back into the house and wrapped his brother's body in one of their blankets. Then he carried the body out toward the grave. He couldn't believe how light it felt, and how it didn't even look like his brother anymore; it looked like a wax effigy. When he reached the grave, he bent over and carefully placed the body at the bottom of the trench. Then he picked up the spade and began covering it with the dark earth. Once he was finished filling in the grave, he took out his penny knife and carved a large and jagged E into a flat stone. Then he placed it at the head of the mound.

Job went back inside their dwelling and looked through their small cupboards. Inside one of them, hidden beneath some old rags, he found a weathered cigar box containing some of his brother's things. At the bottom of the box beneath his grandfather's tattered black bandanna, he found a creased and yellowing envelope. He opened it and found a letter he assumed was the one Eli had spoken about, though the ink had bled to the point of the words being illegible. There was also a photograph of their mother outside a factory with some other young women. In the photograph, his mother's hair was sandy brown like his and was cut short, and the look of defiance he'd vaguely remembered her having was no longer there. There was a sign on the side of the building, too, but it was written in Chinese.

Job went through the rest of the box and found what was left of the family Bible, which his grandfather had used to teach him and Eli to read with and which only included the latter portions of the Old Testament from Ezra to Malachi and the first four books of the New Testament. The salmon-edged pages were folded over in half, and the bundle was fastened together with a strap of leather. He also found the thin, gold wedding band that had belonged to his mother. On a number of occasions, Eli had told him that they should sell it, but Job had steadfastly refused him, and after a while, Eli eventually dropped the matter.

After Job took the letters, photograph, and ring, he put the box aside and opened a worn trunk. In it he found an old blanket, which he laid on the cold earth and folded a few times in order to make a bed roll. Before he rolled it up, he gathered the things he would bring with him. His penny knife. A frayed toothbrush. The bandanna. An empty plastic bottle for water. A beaded metal chain. Three greasy pieces of paper money, folded into tight triangles. Migrant things, things of currency and of necessity. He put everything but the penny knife, money, and chain into the bedroll and then rolled it up and tied it closed with the chain. Then he put the penny knife and money into his pocket.

He left the shack and walked across the village to Old Lady Simons's place, but he would not go inside. He waited until he saw a young girl approaching, then stopped her and gave her one of his bills and asked her to go in and buy him some peanuts.

"Why don't you buy 'em yourself?" she asked.

"That don't concern you," he said. "Now go on, get."

The girl shook her head but took his money and went inside, and after a moment, she came back out with three bags of nuts for him. He took them from her and took his change and then went on his way. Before leaving the village, he stopped at the trailer where the girl with Down syndrome lived. She was sitting outside and rocking back and forth on an empty milk crate, singing some old folk song; her puffy jacket seemed impossibly new and colorful and out of place in their ramshackle surroundings.

Job approached the girl.

"Your brother's over in China, isn't he?" he asked.

The girl looked up at Job with vacant and glassy eyes but said nothing. Job repeated the question.

"I said your brother's in China, right?"

The girl's answer came thickened and wrecked by macroglossia.

"Uh-huh."

"You know how a person goes about getting over there?"

"Uh-uh."

"You know anyone who does?"

Before the girl could reply, a woman spoke from the shack next door.

"There's a woman down in Oakland named Sister Vy."

Job turned to face the woman.

"She takes people over," said the woman, then added, ominously: "For a fee."

"You got a number, or an address?"

"How old are you?"

"Old enough."

The woman studied Job's face before responding.

43

"What's your brother think about this?" she said.

Job nodded toward the clearing.

"You want to ask him, go ahead," he said.

The woman looked toward the freshly mounded earth in the middle of the clearing before looking back to Job.

"Well?" he said. "You gonna help me or not?"

The woman said nothing and went back inside, and Job watched the girl continue to rock back and forth and sing. She licked her lips and her wide almond eyes looked empty, as if she were in some sort of dull rapture. A moment later, the woman returned with an address written on a scrap of newspaper.

"Here," she said, giving it to Job. "I'd be careful if I was you. I heard stories about folks dying on them ships. One of them Palmer boys got on one and it never made it to China or wherever the hell it was headed."

After folding the piece of newspaper and putting it away, Job thanked the woman and walked off. He then made his way toward the winding dirt road leading away from the village and toward the highway. Just before reaching it, he stopped and looked back at the village and at the copse of trees where the graves were and at the girl rocking back and forth on the milk crate. Everything looked so small and wretched and unfamiliar from a distance, and a sick feeling began to bubble up from the pit of his stomach.

When I was five or six, there was an old woman in our village. Her name was Jayel or Jayla or something and she was older than my grandfather. She had but three ruined teeth left in her mouth, and they looked like rotten little stumps and seemed like they were more in the way of things than they were of any use, but that's sometimes just the way things are. At nights, she used to sit quietly by the big fire in the center of the village and smoke hand-rolled cigarettes made from old newspaper and bits of tobacco chaff and stare off toward the Cascades. Her eyes were covered over with milky-white cataracts and it looked like she was blind, but she wasn't. Either that or all her other senses overcompensated and just made it seem so, but it sure felt like she could see you when her eyes were on you. She hardly spoke, but as is the case with those who don't say much, when she did speak, people would listen to what she said. She usually talked about the old days, when she was living with her family down in California. Her parents worked at the SEZ factories they'd built during the trade wars, making parts for computer tablets and cell phones in places like Hercules and Fontana and Crockett. That was around the time they were ramping up all the fracking and mining and stuff, too, keeping the country afloat by gutting it. Of course, it all ran out pretty quick, and once it did, everyone started blaming each other and they tore the country apart at the seams. California was the first state to leave, followed by New York and Texas, and then a handful of city-states after that. Everything else quickly became backwaters, and people started going over to places like Mexico and China and Africa because that's where all the work was, and because things were getting so good over there that the people there didn't have to do the factory work anymore, or at least they wouldn't for what we were willing to.

A couple of years after she got married, Jayel's husband went over to China looking for work. He ended up in a place called New Shenzhen or something like that and made good money putting together solar panels. More than he was making here, at least, and enough to send some home every month for Jayel and their boys. And it kept going along good like that until he got run over in the street there by some rich factory owner's son. She still ended up with a good bit of money from it all, and when her boys were old enough, they went over there, too, and they ended up staying. They even wanted to bring her over as well, but she didn't want to go. I guess she just figured she was too old and wanted to finish her days in the place she'd come from.

When people in the village would complain about the way things were and talk fondly of the past like things were so much different then and so much better, Jayel would laugh and shake her head and say just give it time. Before long, they'll be moving the factories back here because it'll be cheaper again, and then not long after that, the day will come that things will get so good here again that people won't even want the factory work anymore. It might not be in my lifetime and it might not be in yours, but it's the way it's always been and the way it always will be. The world's just one big breaking wheel, and we all get our turn. You'll see.

She must have died when I was seven or eight, but I still remember her cackle and her milky-white eyes and most of the things she said. The only thing I could never figure out, though, was whether she meant we'll each get our turn spinning the wheel or we'll each get our turn being broken on it.

Or maybe it was that she meant both.

II

Job got to the road just before the sun reached its apex. He looked up the broad highway and then down it. There were no vehicles or people in either direction.

He set off and started walking west in the direction of Salem. After a few miles, a cargo truck appeared behind him, heading in his direction. He turned and tried to wave it down, but it passed by without slowing. He resumed walking, and after another mile, a pickup truck loaded with muskmelons came his way.

Job waved again, and this time the vehicle slowed. When it stopped, he got in the flatbed along with the muskmelons and two other passengers, a scarred older man and a teenager Job assumed was the man's son. As the truck pulled away from the shoulder, Job looked back in the direction he'd come from. For a moment, he could have sworn he saw someone at the top of a ridge, just past the tree line. It looked like a boy with a bow over his shoulder and a dead rabbit in his belt, but when he looked again the boy was gone, and as they drove onward he wondered if the boy had even been there at all.

The pickup truck rattled its way west toward Salem. The other two passengers riding in the flatbed mostly slept, except when they were jarred awake whenever the truck swerved to avoid garbage or bottomed out hitting a pothole. Job stared out at the landscape as it scrolled past, at the tent camps, walled communities, and private militias that patrolled the highway off-ramps. Since he'd last traveled along the highway, the camps seemed to have spread and grown, like stains, and the small walled communities' barriers seemed to have been built thicker and higher. Little else had changed, though, other than a vast quarry he'd remembered that had since filled in with a thick, brackish water.

They arrived in Salem just as the sun was beginning to set. Abandoned factories covered with graffiti stood on the outskirts of the town, sentinels of a dead place whose time had passed. The roads were riddled with holes and cracks and other signs of neglect, and the driver had to slow to a crawl in order to navigate around them.

Job got off at a park in the center of town and walked two blocks to the train station. He'd been to Salem a few times before with his grandfather to sell produce, but that had been years ago, and the outdoor market where they'd sold their vegetables no longer existed. The majority of the storefront windows were boarded up or smashed in and revealed empty spaces or spaces piled high with broken furniture and trash. Most of the stores that were still in business sold things of necessity or bought them back from people or did both. Whatever windows the few open stores had were covered over with steel bars or rolling metal shutters.

He passed by an alleyway where a group of teenagers sat in and on top of an abandoned car upon cinder blocks. Crude homemade tattoos were scrawled across their arms and necks, and steel rings and bars pierced their noses and ears and eyebrows, tribal markings of some violent new age clan. They drank dirty plastic bottles full of homemade alcohol steeped from cooking fuel and inhaled aerosol propellant and toluene and shouted and fought each other and seemed volatile and ready to explode. He gave them a wide berth. When he finally arrived at the train station, he found it empty, other than a few armed soldiers who were employed by the train companies to guard the tracks. The ticketing office was dark, and its front door was locked, and Job found a schedule at a nearby display, noting that the last train to Oakland had already left. There were no other trains leaving or coming that night, and the next train wouldn't depart until seven o'clock the following morning.

He left the train station and walked back toward the center of town. He passed a street vendor working beneath the covered island of a burned-out gas station. A group of sunburned men with grease-stained fingers waited as a Mexican woman cooked scraps of horse and rabbit meat on a blackened grill. A man with a sawed-off shotgun across his lap sat behind her in a faded beach chair, and nearby, a pair of dogs fought over the spoiled contents of an overturned garbage can. Down alleyways, Job could see people cooking around campfires or sitting under thatched roofs or jerry-built shelters made from plastic paneling or corrugated siding. The town looked like ruins to him, and every time he saw its ragged denizens peering out at him from alleyways or from the shacks they were encamped in, a cold shiver ran through his body.

Job soon reached the center of town, but there was nothing open other than a money transfer office guarded by a pair of soldiers and a pawnshop with barred windows displaying an array of jewelry, scuffed power tools, and guns. The farther away he got from the train station, the fewer lights and people there seemed to be. He continued walking and eventually spotted a diner, but when he reached it, he realized that it had been closed for some time. The tables inside were covered with dust or overturned, and the cushions of the booths had been slashed open or ripped out altogether. When he noticed a man in a dirty sweater watching him from a darkened

51

second-floor window across the way, he turned around
and headed back in the direction he'd come from.

When he got back to the train station, he looked
around until he found a restroom. He went inside, and a
motion-sensing light came on and illuminated its graffiti-
covered walls. The restroom stank of mildew and urine
and rust. Distrustful, he checked the three stalls to see if
there was anyone there. Once he was sure he was alone, he
took out the ring from his pocket and removed the beaded
metal chain from the bedroll. He threaded the chain
through the ring and then hung it around his neck and hid
it underneath his shirt. Then he hid his money in his
underwear. Before he left the bathroom, he slipped his
penny knife into his work boot, where it would be easy to
reach.

Out on the platform, he sat on a bench, took off his
bedroll, and put it on the bench next to him. The light
from an overhead fluorescent bulb illuminated the area
and lit up the myriad particulate in the air. The pollution
was so bad that it looked like a light snow was slowly
falling in whatever wan pools of light there were. There
was a faint smell of formaldehyde in the air, and it made
Job's stomach roil whenever he breathed in too deeply.

After he'd sat there for some time, Job reached into
his bedroll and took out one of the bags of peanuts he'd
had the girl buy for him from Old Lady Simons. He
looked at the package, but when he saw how few there
were, he decided to save them until his hunger was more

severe. He put them away and took out the bound pages
of the Bible, even though he'd never been that good of a
reader nor had he been all that interested in its contents.
As a child, he'd preferred his grandfather's tales about the
wars in the Middle East and Africa and the Koreas and
about working on the pipelines and in the mines to the
staid fables of the church. Stories of adventure and of
violence and of excitement rather than morals and
allegory. But he was beginning to feel lonely and was
starting to wish he hadn't left the village, and he wanted
something to take his mind off things, so he began to leaf
through the pages, hoping to find some sort of solace or at
least some diversion. He read a bit from Ecclesiastes about
the simple pleasures of daily life, like eating and drinking
and taking one's portion, but these things only made him
even hungrier and lonelier, so he flipped ahead and read
some from the Book of Isaiah. He found the songs of the
suffering servants interesting and there were some
exciting parts about chariots and slaying one's enemies in
battle, but all the passages about bondage and captivity
just made him feel sad again and made him think of his
mother in some vague factory somewhere, so he closed the
book and just sat there staring off toward the hazy
polluted skies and wondering what it was like back in the
village. He was so deep in thought that he hardly even
heard it when the woman spoke.

"Heading south?" she asked.

53

Job looked up and saw a woman in her midtwenties standing nearby, holding a stained duffel bag. She wore long skirts, some sort of scuffed riding boots, and a man's jacket, and she had a nest of wiry strawberry hair underneath a knit woolen cap. At first, he wasn't sure if she was real or if she was from a dream he might've been having.

"I'm not bothering you, am I?" asked the woman.

"No."

"'Cause if I am, I can just leave you alone."

He said nothing and watched as she took out a dirty plastic bag full of tobacco scraps and newspaper and rolled a cigarette as thin as a toothpick. As she licked the edge of the newspaper and pressed it shut, he wondered how long she'd been standing there watching him and where she'd come from and, perhaps more importantly, what she wanted. When she was finished rolling the cigarette, she offered it to him.

"You smoke?"

He shook his head.

"That's good," she said. "I'd quit myself, but what's the point? Ain't like the air's much cleaner."

She laughed hoarsely at her own joke, lit the cigarette with a match, and took a deep drag. He started to grow uncomfortable; being around someone he knew nothing about made him uneasy. Halfway through exhaling, she spoke again.

"You hear the one about the science experiment?"

He shook his head.

"A class did an experiment with some worms," she said. "First one they put in a jar of alcohol. Next one they put in a jar of smoke. The third one they put in a jar of come, and the fourth one they put in a jar of dirt. After a couple days, they checked them, and they were all dead except the one in the dirt. So the teacher asked the class 'What can you learn from this?' and one of the students said, 'As long as you drink and smoke and screw, you won't end up with worms.'"

When she finished telling the joke, she laughed again and shook her head.

"You do know what come is, don't you?" she said.

"Course I do," he said, angry.

"Well," she said. "I think it's funny."

He didn't reply.

"You don't talk much, do you?" she said.

Again, he didn't speak, still gauging the situation. "Still waters run deep, huh?" she said.

She smiled again, revealing her despoiled teeth, and he began to feel sick. He felt uncertain and exposed, as if he were tracking an animal he knew nothing about and wasn't sure how it attacked or what made it attack or what its strengths and weaknesses were. She took another long drag from the cigarette and then slowly exhaled through her nose. Then she looked up and down the platform.

"Ain't you a little young to be traveling alone?" she asked.

He felt his insides curdle, and he tensed up.

"Who said I was alone?" he said.

"There I go, bothering you again," she said. "I just saw you reading the good book, and being a fellow traveler and all, I thought you looked like you could use some company. I didn't mean nothing by it."

He didn't reply, and he felt the queasiness spreading through the pit of his stomach.

"Tell you what," she said. "I'm gonna leave now, but if you feel like some company, me and a friend are over there in the park. You see her there?"

She pointed to a park studded with desiccated broom bushes and wilted rhododendrons, where a woman stood warming her hands by a small fire.

"We're waiting for the train, too," she said. "Lessie's making a stew, and her stews are just about as good as they get. Come by if you get hungry. We don't bite."

She took one last drag and flicked the cigarette butt toward the tracks and then left without waiting for a reply. Job watched her walk off toward the park. Then he looked up and down the tracks. There were no lights in sight, and in both directions, he felt like he was staring down a deep and darkened well.

Job sat there on the bench for a few more hours. He read some more of the Book of Isaiah and counted the cracks in the pavement and just stared at the light. Occasionally, he glanced over at the small fire in the park. Every time he looked, the women were sitting there, talking and laughing and spooning stew from empty soda cans cut in half. They didn't seem threatening at all, but he was still reticent to trust anyone.

When midnight approached, he began to nod off. He retied the pages of the Bible with the leather strap and held them off to his side so they'd drop if he started to fall asleep, and the sound of them hitting the pavement would wake him. He looked toward the fire again and then looked toward the phosphorescent lights of the cities to the south. The incandescing glow above the horizon looked like the outline of a giant slumbering dragon or a hazy mountain that was somehow aflame.

As he nodded off, he thought of the Willamette Valley. He thought of their village, and of the murky river that coursed past it. He floated over it all fast and low like a diving hawk and then circled high above it before diving back down again.

Before long, he woke with a start when he heard his Bible slap against the concrete. As he glanced around and got his bearings, he saw the empty tracks and the darkened station house. Then he saw a man watching him from the platform across the way. He recognized the man as the one with the dirty sweater who'd been watching him from the darkened window back in town. It was impossible to know how long the man had been standing there, but it was clear that the man was studying him.

Job looked back toward the park where the two women huddled around the small fire. Their fire had diminished in size, but it was still burning brightly in the grimy night. Then he glanced back at the man across the tracks. The man looked off when their gazes met. Something didn't feel right about him; he had no luggage, and he didn't look like he was going anywhere. Job picked up his bedroll and the Bible, then got up and made his way toward the park. When he approached the fire, the woman with the strawberry hair looked up at him.

"Well, well," she said. "I didn't think you were gonna come over."

"You mind?"

"Not at all. Have a seat."

He sat down across from them, keeping his distance in case something happened. In the near darkness, the woman with the strawberry hair appeared more attractive than she'd appeared under the bright light of the platform. Or perhaps it was just the small amount of familiarity she now provided that made her seem that way. He could hardly see her teeth or the peeling skin on her nose, and the shadows made her cheekbones more angular and prominent. The other woman was dark-haired and overweight, but she seemed friendly if a little slow.

"Want some stew?" asked the woman with the strawberry hair.

"No, thanks."

"You sure? It's really good. There's squirrel in it, right, Lessie?"

The other woman nodded. It smelled good and he was hungry, but he was uncomfortable taking food from people he didn't know, so he shook his head.

"Well, if you change your mind just say the word," she said. "Now where was I?"

"You were talking about your friend, Ariel," said Lessie.

"Oh, yeah. She always seems to be in the right place at the right time. Just got hired as a helper for some wealthy Chinese family in the free state of San Francisco. Even gets to live in their house and gets every other Sunday off."

"No kidding?"

"Some people in this life are just plain lucky. They just always seem to land in the right place at the right time. Then there are others who just can't even catch a break even if they have more going for them. It's like they're just cursed or something."

"I hope I end up with a good job like that," said Lessie. "I'd work for a Chinese family, or any family, for that matter."

"Well, don't hold your breath."

The woman with the strawberry hair leaned over the fire and refilled her halved soda can with stew. Job got a whiff of it from across the way, and it smelled salty and fatty and delicious.

"You sure you don't want some?" she asked.

He hesitated.

"It's really good. I'd almost think it was steak or something if I didn't know any better."

He felt his empty stomach growling like a pack of dogs. After a moment, he moved closer to the fire.

"Well," he said. "Maybe I'll have just a little."

They talked into the night. Job finished the can of stew they gave him and promised to himself that he wasn't going to have any more, but it was so rich and tasty, and it'd been so long since he'd eaten any meat that when they offered him more, he couldn't help but say yes.

The women talked about their travels and about the jobs they'd had and the places they'd seen and the people they'd met. He rarely interjected and mostly listened or gave brief answers when they asked him questions. He occasionally glanced around looking for the man with the dirty sweater who'd been following him, but eventually stopped when it appeared that the man was gone. Every now and then, he glanced over at the train station as well, but no one else had come since he left and there were no signs of any activity there.

The woman with the strawberry hair, whose name was Maddison, talked about working in the desert's battery factories with her mother when she was little. She talked about running away as a teenager and making fast money in the brothels in the free state of San Francisco before getting her face slashed up by a drunken client. No one wanted to sleep with her after that, and she'd gone back to the SEZ factories to look for work, but all the work was gone, and she'd ended up getting hired by a fracking company up north and made good money for a while until there wasn't any gas left in the ground. Since then, she'd been drifting, doing odd jobs up and down the coastline. Lessie talked about her life, and how she'd been born in the city-state of DC and how she'd been given up at birth and how she'd run away from an orphanage when she was eleven because there was no food there and the man running the orphanage could not keep his hands off his charges. She talked about the farms and mines and factories she'd worked at, and the brief marriage she'd had to a man from AlLoMi, the confederacy of Alabama, Louisiana, and Mississippi, before they'd lost touch after he'd gone to Brazil in search of work. She didn't know if the man was still alive or if he was dead and had long since given up trying to find out. They were stories of restlessness and adventure and heartbreak and regeneration, and even though Job felt like he was at the beginning of his own story somehow, he had a vague and unsettling premonition that the only difference between he and them was that he was at an earlier stage of a similar journey.

After a while, Job started to grow tired again, but it was a different kind of tired than he was used to; it was a kind that started at the base of his skull and radiated outward in all directions in slow battering waves and that no amount of willpower would allow him to stave off. He began to feel sluggish and warm and almost giddy, like the time he and Eli had drunk a jar of cloudy spirits they'd found in a forest cave. Shapes began to distort and grow long or contract, and lights grew blurry or blinding and the sounds of the women's voices began to screech and swirl around him as if he were in a centrifuge. He almost retched, but he somehow managed to keep down the contents of his stomach.

Maddison turned to face him.

"You all right?" she asked.

He nodded.

"You sure?"

He nodded again and swatted for purchase, but there was nothing within reach.

"You want some water or something?" she asked.

He shook his head and fought his way to his feet, inwardly cursing himself for eating their stew. The fire spun before him like a Catherine wheel and the ground beneath tilted as if it were the deck of a ship upon a rough sea. Maddison stood.

"Let me give you a hand," she said.

As she approached him, he shoved her out of the way and staggered forward through the glowering coals. He kicked over the pot of stew, and his mismatched boots kicked up storms of bright red sparks.

"Careful there," said Maddison.

Lessie stood, too, and they followed him as he staggered toward a cluster of broom bushes.

"Hey," said Lessie.

"Leave me alone," he said.

They tried to help him, but he shoved them away.

"Easy there—"

After he pulled free, he lurched forward a few more steps. Then he stumbled and collapsed face first into the mud.

The last thing he heard before he passed out was Maddison telling Lessie to give her a hand. Then everything went black and he felt like he was falling through space. The blood pumped hot and warm in his heart and in his ears, and the farther he fell, the farther away their voices got, and a part of him wanted to just keep falling until it all disappeared into a warm, soft, black nothingness. But another part of him, a deeper and more primal and wordless part attuned to instinct and survival, knew that that would be a mistake and clamored at him like a great thundering bell to open his eyes and to get up and fight before it was too late.

When he finally came to, Job found himself on his back in the mud underneath the long, drooping fingers of a dying rhododendron. The two women were rifling through his pockets, and the man in the dirty sweater was going through his bedroll nearby. Job's lace-up boot was half-untied, and the jodhpur boot was gone, and he felt dizzy and nauseous.

"Hey," said Lessie. "I think he's awake."

Job struggled to an unsteady crouch. They tried to hold him down, but he slapped away their hands and scrambled away from them.

"I thought you gave him the stuff?" asked the man. He had a lemon-sized tumor covered with ingrown hairs on the side of his neck, and he cringed and spat out the words when he spoke.

"We did give him the stuff," said Maddison.

"Well, you didn't give him enough, now, did you?"

The man dropped the bedroll and lunged for Job, but Job reached down for the penny knife in his work boot, yanked it out, and clumsily jabbed it at him.

"Easy, boy," said the man.

"Stay back," said Job, his tongue dumb and slow.

"We just want your money. It ain't nothing personal."

The three of them fanned out before continuing to advance toward Job from separate directions. Job stabbed out at the air again with the penny knife; he saw two of each of them.

"I said stay back," he said.

"Don't be stupid—"

The man lunged for Job, but Job sidestepped him and pushed his way past. When Maddison came next, he grabbed her by the wrist and twisted it behind her back and into an armlock. As Lessie took a step toward him, Job put the blade to Maddison's throat.

"That's far enough," he said.

Lessie froze.

"Give me my stuff," said Job.

"Hang on a second—"

Job pushed the tip of the blade into the flesh of Maddison's neck until it drew blood.

"I said give me my stuff," he said.

"You heard him," said Maddison.

Lessie picked up Job's bedroll and tossed it to him, and he slung it over his shoulder. Still holding the knife to Maddison's throat, Job began to back up toward the train station. He could feel his heart hammering in his chest and in his ears and in his throat.

"Stay where you are," he said.

The other two watched as Job slowly backed away, staring at him like vultures and waiting for him to fall. He was still weak and dizzy from whatever it was they'd given him, and he took each step carefully and with great deliberation. At one point, he stepped on a piece of glass with his bare foot, and it cut into his heel and made him stumble, but he righted himself and continued on and somehow made it all the way to the station. Once he got there, Maddison tried to turn and face him, and he could smell her sour breath when she spoke. He looked around for the armed soldiers who'd been guarding the station, but they were nowhere to be seen.

"Where you taking me?" she asked.

"Shut up."

She tried to pull free from him, but he twisted her arm up higher and pushed the tip of the blade deeper into the soft flesh of her throat.

"Come on," she said. "Let's talk this over."

"Ain't nothing to talk about."

"What happened back there wasn't my doing. Honest."

Job stumbled again and nearly fell when he stepped down with his bare foot onto a sharp piece of metal. The adrenaline was diminishing and the effects of whatever they'd given him were coming back, so he tightened his grip on her and trudged onward.

"Look, I know we got off to a bad start, but it ain't what you think," she said.

He didn't reply.

"What do you say you and I go off together?" she said.

"Forget it."

He turned and spotted the restroom about fifty feet away.

"I can help you," she said. "I've been down south. Out east. Been all over."

"I ain't going nowhere with you."

"There's things I know. Things I can teach you."

He shut his eyes and tried to quell the vertigo that was threatening to overtake him.

"You can fuck me, too," she said. "I've got a tight pussy, and it's clean."

"Shut up."

"Please—"

Before she could finish, he shoved her to the ground and then turned and staggered the last few feet into the bathroom. Once inside, he shut the door behind him and yanked down one of the stall doors and wedged it between the door and the wall. Maddison pounded on the other side of the door, but his brace held, and he bolstered it with a garbage can. She shouted from the other side.

"Open this door, you little fucker!"

He staggered over to one of the sinks and promptly vomited into it. Bits of blackened bile studded the thick mess that came forth. Maddison continued to pound against the door, but the makeshift brace held.

"Open up," she said.

"Go away," he croaked.

He vomited again and continued to throw up until he had nothing left to give and then he dry heaved a few times before finally collapsing to the floor. Maddison continued to shout at him from the other side of the door.

"You dumb son of a bitch," she said. "I could've helped you. You're gonna regret this. You'll see! Oh yeah, you'll see!"

Job soon slept, and when he slept, he had no dreams. When he woke, he found himself in the same position he'd fallen asleep in. Though the lights were off, a dull and milky glow steeped through one of the bathroom's wire-reinforced windows. The tiles he lay upon were cold and wicked with moisture, and his bare foot throbbed and the bottom of it was scabbed with a skein of dried blood.

Job pushed himself instinctively into a crouch and spun around and looked toward the door. The motion-sensing lights came back on and he saw that the section of stall door bracing it was bent, but it had somehow held. As he stood, a wave of vertigo washed over him and made his knees buckle. He reached out for the sink to steady himself and almost slipped on the cold porcelain; his head buzzed like a nest of angry yellow jackets, and his mouth was as dry as wool. The last thing he remembered was Maddison shouting through the door at him, and he couldn't remember when he had passed out or fallen asleep.

He turned on the faucet, but no water came forth. The bottom of the sink was crusted with his dried vomit. He saw the open penny knife lying on the floor and picked it up and closed it before slipping it back into his boot. Then he checked to see if the ring was still hanging from his neck. Once he felt it with his fingers, he checked his underwear for his money and found that as well.

After fashioning a makeshift shoe for his bare foot with the tattered bandanna and a section of the Bible for a sole, he climbed up onto one of the sinks and pulled himself up to peer through a window. Though the hammered glass obfuscated the images outside, he could see that the sun was up and that there were a number of shapes moving out on the platform. He climbed back down and retied his bedroll and slung it over his shoulder. After taking a deep breath, he removed the brace. Then he slowly opened the door.

Outside, it was warm and humid even though the sun was barely up. The sky was choked with so much chemical haze that distances were impossible to reckon. Job scanned the surroundings for any sign of his assailants, but he found none. At some point during the night, they must've found someone else to rob or had given up and left.

He made his way toward the ticketing office. Two armed soldiers patrolled the tracks near the station, and a clerk sat inside the office behind another wire-reinforced window. The man's egg-shaped head was plastered with thin greasy strands of hair, and he was reading a tablet computer's screen and didn't look up when Job approached the window.

Job asked for a one-way ticket to Oakland. After the man printed the ticket, Job paid for it with nearly all of the money he had left. Then he made his way over to the platform, where a scattering of passengers waited. A young man whose right ear was missing sat on a bench with a canvas bag at his feet, and a pair of scantily dressed and heavily made-up teens pointed at Job's makeshift shoe and whispered to each other, laughing.

He stood on the platform and waited for the train. It arrived at the station a few minutes later, and no one got off. Job filed onto the train after the others did and headed toward the rear. He passed some sleeping migrants, a man in an ill-fitting wool suit, and a young woman who clutched her possessions tightly to her like a pregnant woman holding her swollen belly. He found an open window seat by the back of the car and sat down, then stared out at Salem as he waited for the train to leave the station. He only saw two people outside, an armed train guard and an old woman pushing a rusty shopping cart stuffed with her dirty possessions. Other than that, the town looked like a cemetery.

A whistle blew outside by the front of the train, and one last passenger hurried toward the train and climbed aboard just before its doors closed. A moment later, the train jerked forward and slowly pulled away from the station. Before long, they were outside the city, and its run-down outskirts, abandoned factories, and migrant camps quickly receded into the distance.

They reached Eugene by midmorning, and the train chuffed its way farther south, past Lorane and Yoncalla and Sutherlin. At each stop, more passengers climbed on board. Most of them were shabby and anonymous young men and women; they traveled alone or in small groups and carried everything they owned in large polypropylene sacks and duffel bags or in their pockets and on their backs. They wore knockoff jeans and puffy jackets or secondhand suits, and they left dying villages, rural backwaters, and small towns for the SEZs in the south and the port cities of Oakland and New San Diego and Galveston IV and Tijuana. There was an occasional family or married couple, but most of the passengers traveled alone; it was far too difficult to find food and shelter and work for one person much less an entire family, and those who traveled fast traveled light.

As the cars filled, passengers began to sit out in the aisles and on the floors. They were mostly country people and were used to living communally and out in the open. Some took off their shoes and rubbed their feet or picked at the dried skin on their heels. Others ate salted melon seeds or hard-boiled eggs or shucked peanuts and dropped the trash onto the floor. One slight young man wedged himself up on the overhead luggage rack and slept there like a possum; another stretched out upon the floor. Others formed groups and chatted excitedly, sharing rumors and information about factories in other countries or how to secure passage abroad or cities or factories to avoid. Nearly all of the conversations were centered around survival and necessity and work.

The closer they got to Oakland, the better off and more experienced the boarding travelers appeared to be.

Some even had cell phones, and before long, loud and annoying ring tones began to puncture the air, chirping snippets of hackneyed classical music or the choruses of popular songs. Industrious vendors came aboard the cars and fought their way through the swelling crowds, selling hot dogs and vape pens and bottled water and bootleg antibiotics. Others passed around leaflets advertising rooms for rent in Oakland and Chinese and Spanish lessons and places that sold anything and everything a traveler could need. The cars slowly transformed from tiny rural villages into buzzing hives of commerce and industry and prepared the passengers for what was to come. There was an electric feeling of excitement and possibility and hope in the air, and it grew and compounded with each additional passenger and each additional mile.

Job stared out the window and watched the scrolling landscape pass by, staring in wonder at the gutted quarries and the sprawling shantytowns and the landfills that seemed to have no ends. He was already as far from home as he'd ever been, and he couldn't believe it had only been twenty-four hours since he'd left the village. So much had happened so quickly, and it was all so new and dangerous and exciting and raw. Though he missed the village and his brother, he was excited for what was to come; he watched in wide-eyed awe as the dying clear-cut forests and strip-mined mountaintops slowly gave way to arid wastelands full of abandoned SEZ factories and closed-down power plants, and then he watched as those gave way to endless stretches of run-down and empty exurbs and suburbs and small towns and cities.

As they continued on, he took in the theater happening all around him. In the next row, a relationship blossomed between a pair of teenagers from different villages; in the row after that, a mother breastfed a diaper-less child wearing a soiled T-shirt. In the seats across from Job, a woman studied a battered and dog-eared Chinese textbook while another watched violent cartoons on a smartphone. Out in the aisle, Job observed a pickpocket snatch the thin wallet of an unsuspecting passenger before continuing on his way toward the next car.

The cars swelled with more and more people as the train rode farther south. They sat or stood in the aisles and piled into the seats and crammed into the luggage racks. Those who traveled with others or found friends got them to keep their seats as they fought their way toward squalid restrooms. Those who had no one to do this held it in or took their possessions with them, knowing the seats would no longer be free when they returned.

At one point, a young woman squeezed into the seat across from Job when the person who was sitting there got up to leave. She smiled at Job, but he ignored her and kept to himself. As the day gave way to night, those who could slept fitfully wherever they were; those who could not continued to talk or eat or watch things on their smartphones as if it were the middle of the day. Job was too excited to sleep and too restless to read, so he just continued to stare out at the darkened landscape as it went by.

Shortly before dawn, they made their first stop of the day and pulled into Martinez. One person fought his way through the masses to get off the train while everyone else stayed aboard. Another dozen crammed onto the car even though there was hardly any room, and they jostled together like bottles in a crate as the train lurched onward. Outside, the sun soon rose above the horizon behind a blanket of smog and began to brighten the chalky sky.

As the train approached El Cerrito and New Beijing, Job began to make out the walled city-state of San Francisco in the distance, across the bay. At first, he could not believe the enormity of it; buildings as high as mountains climbed toward the heavens. It was a completely artificial and man-made landscape and unlike anything Job had ever seen, and it was both awesome and horrifying at the same time.

A few more passengers got out at Berkeley before the train curled southeastward toward Oakland's main terminal; a handful more got on and took their places among the others. As the train approached its final stop, the passengers gathered their belongings and put on their jackets and shoes and began preparing to disembark. Those who had befriended each other made vague promises to meet again or exchanged cell phone numbers or addresses if they had them or said good lucks and good-byes. Others edged into the aisles or bottled up around the exits. A pressure was building up all around Job, and it was so palpable that he could feel it as if there had been a change in the barometric pressure or the humidity.

When the train finally reached the city, it dipped below the earth and went underground like some giant snake returning to its burrow. Everything went black for a few seconds before the lights of the car finally flickered on. After another moment, the train emerged from the tunnel and approached the main station. The last few passengers who were still seated rose and stood with the others. Job stood as well and shoved his hands deep into his pockets to protect his meager possessions. There were people all around him, and he felt them shoving him and elbowing him and pressing up against him. He could feel their warmth and their rough clothing, and he could smell their body odor and rank breath.

The train pulled into the station and began to slow. At the end of the tracks, it lurched to a stop and briefly shuddered and then went still. Everyone paused for a moment and then waited restlessly until the doors opened. Once they finally did, the mass of bodies surged through them and spilled out into the station.

Job fought his way through the packed terminal. He'd never been around so many people before, and in such a tight space, and he found it terrifying. He eventually found an exit and went up a stairwell and made his way outside. The streets surrounding the station were a further hive of activity; entrepreneurial locals peddled items geared toward the needs of arriving migrants and those heading to other countries. Toothbrushes and soap. Tickets for cargo ships. Job placement services. Temporary rooms to share. A number of merchants traded currency or medications while still others offered knockoff jeans and respirators and refurbished tablets and phones.

He made his way away from the station and into the city. He occasionally glanced up at the sky, but he couldn't see anything but thick, gray haze. The air around him was full of dust and made his eyes water so much that he had to squint. Somewhere overhead there were jets flying past, but the pollution was so thick that he couldn't see them and could only hear the faint rumblings of their engines.

When he reached the street, Job watched someone flag down a self-driving vehicle. He tried doing the same with no success and then saw someone else using a cell phone to access another self-driving vehicle. He soon noticed a dilapidated human-driven vehicle and tried to get the driver's attention, but the driver drove by without slowing. Seeing another human-driven vehicle, Job stepped out into the street and waved down the driver. The driver pulled to the curb, and Job tried to get in the front door of the vehicle, but the driver motioned toward the back door with his thumb.

Job got in backseat, and the driver looked to him through the reflection of the rearview mirror. A thick, scuffed plastic shield separated the front of the car from the back. Realizing the driver was waiting for a destination, Job took out the piece of newspaper the woman in his village had given him and read the address. Without replying, the driver pulled the taxi away from the curb and into traffic. While they drove through the city, Job took in his surroundings. He saw garbage in every direction he looked; there were empty wrappers and bottles and cans and discarded furniture and broken hunks of Styrofoam. People lived in dirty and cramped shacks that had no plumbing or electricity and were cobbled together with cinder blocks and plywood and corrugated metal siding. Some pulled carts full of junk along the sides of the streets while others rode two and three and even four to a moped. Outside the buildings that weren't run down, armed guards stood watch before barricaded checkpoints, letting gleaming vehicles in and out of the subterranean garages' entrances.

Before long, the driver pulled the taxi to the curb outside a store at the edge of a block of run-down apartment buildings. Job paid the driver with the last of his money and got out. He watched the vehicle go and then approached the store. After he compared the address on the scrap of paper to the address on the door, he went inside. A mechanism on the arm of the door set off the tinkling chimes of an electronic bell. At a counter in the back of the store, a burly young man wearing dark sunglasses stared in Job's direction. He spoke in a language Job couldn't make out; sleeves of colorful koi fish and dragons snaked up his muscular arms.

"Hello?" said Job, making his way back toward the counter.

The man continued to chatter at Job in some unrecognizable tongue.

"I beg your pardon—?"

Before Job could finish, the man took off the sunglasses, revealing images of another person on the insides of the lenses, which appeared to be tiny video screens. The man glared at Job, angry at him for interrupting his conversation. He seemed to be wearing some sort of contact lenses that made him appear feline.

"What do you want?" he said.

"I'm looking for Sister Vy," said Job.

"Don't know no Sister Vy."

"I was told I could find her here—"

The man interrupted him and put back on his sunglasses.

"You were told wrong," he said.

"You know where I can find her?"

"Get out of here."

Job hesitated.

"You deaf?" said the young man. "I said get the fuck out of here."

After a moment, Job turned and left the store. Outside, he looked up the street. Then he looked back in the direction he'd come from. He thought about his brother's grave and the stale taste of bay nuts and the way it got bone cold in their shack during the winter. Then he took a deep breath and went back inside. As the mechanism on the arm of the door set off the chimes again, the young man looked up and saw Job approaching again and he again took off his sunglasses.

"I need to see Sister Vy," said Job.

"I told you to fuck off—"

Job interrupted him, pulling out the ring on the chain around his neck.

"I have money," he said. "I have this, too."

The young man came out from behind the counter and grabbed Job by the neck and began to drag him toward the door.

"Please," said Job.

Before the young man could reply, a pinched female voice came over an intercom.

"Wait," it said.

The young man froze and looked up toward the video camera. After a moment, the voice over the intercom continued.

"Bring him back to me."

Job was brought up a narrow stairwell and down a
hallway and then through a locked steel door into a small
and windowless room. Inside the room, a middle-aged
woman with cropped gray hair and narrow eyes behind
thick glasses sat at a desk, tallying figures in a green
ledger. She wore simple clothes, and she was short and
solid and built like a bulldog; were it not for her small and
sagging breasts, one might've thought she was asexual.
She was beyond anonymous almost to the point of being
invisible; her voice was calm and matronly yet undeniably
authoritative, and she spoke without looking up.

"Leave us, Ramon," she said.

The young man left and closed the door behind him,
and when it closed, it locked into place. As Job stood there,
the woman finally looked up and looked him over as if she
was inspecting a side of beef.

"How did you hear about me?" she asked.

"You helped someone from our village," said Job.

"What village?"

"Ellendale."

The woman said nothing.

"It's in Oregon," said Job. "By the Willamette."

"I know where it is."

Job said nothing.

"The Mozers are from Ellendale, aren't they?" said
the woman.

"Yes, ma'am," said Job.

"You'll have to excuse my associate. We've been having some problems with the authorities."

The woman opened a small packet of what looked like mints, took one out, and carefully placed it onto her tongue before continuing.

"So I take it you want to go over?" she asked.

"Yes, ma'am."

"You sure about that?"

He nodded.

"How old are you?"

"Eighteen."

"You hardly look twelve. Tell me how old you really are, and don't lie."

"Fourteen."

"I don't transport children—"

He interrupted her.

"I'm not a child," he said.

"Your parents know about this?"

"I don't have any."

"You have any money?"

"I have this."

He removed the chain with the ring on it from his neck and handed it to her. She looked it over.

"It's gold," he said.

"Even if it is, how do you plan on paying the balance? A ring like this will barely even cover a down payment."

"I'll find a way."

"You have anyone over there?"

"My mother."

"I thought you said you didn't have parents?"

"She went over when I was little."

"You got anyone else?"

He shook his head. The woman pursed her lips but said nothing.

"I'll work it off," said Job. "I promise."

The woman took off her glasses and wiped them with a small cloth before continuing.

"I need someone to help the ship's crew," she said. "Cleaning latrines and that sort of thing. You'll still have to cover the balance once you get over there. We're talking about a year or two's work, maybe more."

"Okay."

"You try to run off without paying, you'll end up in a ditch somewhere with your hands cut off and your teeth pulled out."

"I won't."

She took the ring off the chain before returning the chain to him.

"I'll hold onto this," she said. "Assuming it's real, I can put you on a ship in a few days."

The woman flipped a switch underneath the desk, and after a moment, the door opened. She nodded to Ramon, who appeared to have been waiting outside the entire time.

"Chip him, and get him some shoes," she said.

"Thanks," said Job, standing.

"Don't thank me. I'm just protecting my investment."

Before Job could reply, Ramon pulled him into the hallway. As the woman went back to studying the figures in the ledger, the door to the office slowly clanged shut.

They walked downstairs and into an underground garage. Ramon led Job to an equipment closet and unlocked it, then briefly went inside and reappeared a moment later with what looked like a pistol. Job took a quick step backward, but Ramon grabbed Job's neck before he could squirm away.

"Relax," he said.

Before Job could react, Ramon pointed the pistol against the space in between Job's shoulder blades and squeezed the trigger. There was no sound, but Job felt a sharp and painful prick.

"Now we'll know where you are if you try to run," said Ramon.

Job rubbed the sore spot between his shoulder blades as Ramon put the device back in the storage closet. It felt like there was a lentil beneath his skin. They left the garage, and Ramon drove Job to a warehouse that stood across from what Job assumed to be an abandoned pet food factory, from the faded picture of a happy-looking Labrador retriever on its side. Ramon unlocked a thick padlock on a rolling steel door to the warehouse and then raised the door so they could go in. After they went in and

Ramon rolled down and relocked the door from the inside, it occurred to Job that the people who were already there were locked in like animals in a cage. Before he could say anything, though, Ramon shoved him toward a stairwell.

"Keep moving," he said.

Job entered the stairwell and started up the stairs. The thin soles of the cheap boat shoes Ramon had given him squeaked as he went. There wasn't much light inside the stairwell, and it smelled faintly of stale dog kibble. On the fourth floor, they left the stairwell and went out into a large open room illuminated by a few naked fluorescent bulbs.

Job glanced around at the surroundings. Inside the large room, two dozen people lay on barren mattresses on bunk beds or sat at wooden benches and tables, playing cards and reading magazines. Though there were a couple of families and younger women traveling alone, the majority of the occupants were men in their late teens and twenties and early thirties. Some were white; some weren't. Some looked like they came from the city; others looked like they came from rural villages, like Job's. A few were dressed in plain black suits or sweaters and khakis, but most wore sweatshirts and jeans or track pants.

"Find a bed," said Ramon. "You need to use the bathroom, there's one down the hall."

Before Job could reply, Ramon walked off, closing and locking the door behind him. Job went forward and approached one of the rows of beds. He found an unoccupied mattress near the end of one row, but when he went to put down his bedroll, someone spoke behind him.

"That one's taken."

Job turned to see a trio of hardened young men. They wore black and had crude tattoos on their thin, chiseled arms, and they looked Filipino or some other mixture of Latino and Asian.

"Sorry?"

The leader of the trio spoke again, revealing gold dental grills on his teeth. The name "CRUZE" was tattooed across his neck.

"I said that one's taken," he said.

Job picked up his bedroll and moved to the next unoccupied bed, but when he went to set his bedroll down, Cruze spoke again.

"That one's taken, too."

Job picked up his bedroll again and moved on to the next unoccupied bed, but Cruze spoke again before he could put his things down.

"So's that one."

"You want to tell me which ones aren't?"

"If I were you, I'd sleep out in the shitter. Should be more like what you're used to, you fucking hick."

Job clenched his fists, but Cruze moved toward Job and got close to his face.

"You got something you want to say to me?" he said.

Job hesitated.

"Do him," said one of the other young men.

Cruze was so close to him that Job could smell his sour and smoky breath. He continued to hesitate, and after a moment, Cruze spoke.

"That's what I thought," he said.

Someone else spoke from the bunks that were a few rows away.

"There's an open one over here."

Job turned to see an overweight boy a few years older than him reading on the lower berth of a bunk bed at the end of another row. The boy wore thick glasses, baggy jeans, and a hooded sweatshirt, and judging by his pudginess, healthy hair, and lack of scars, he seemed somehow better off than the others.

"Go on with fatty," said Cruze. "You bitches make a good pair."

Job ignored them both and moved on to another row. He found an empty bed, and then he quietly began to put away his things.

Ramon returned to the warehouse at night with bananas and lunchmeat and some jugs of water and a few loaves of stale bread. Those who were staying there gathered around him and pleaded and fought for position as he passed out the food. There was barely enough to go around, and the first and strongest ones got the most while the others got what little was left or nothing at all.

Job managed to get a few slices of bread. The overweight boy got a few of the bananas, and they ended up sitting near each other at the end of one of the tables and sharing with each other. For a while, they ate in silence, but the overweight boy kept starting conversations, and though Job said little, the overweight boy talked enough for them both. His name was Cleary and he was eighteen; he was from the free state of Texas and had recently gotten into one of the universities there, but a government official had stolen his identity so he could enroll his own son in Cleary's place. Though his father ran a small processing plant, he had little influence with the government, so he was sending Cleary to China to stay with an uncle until he could get into a university there. He was polite enough though clingy, and he seemed to think his chances were better if he was with Job than on his own.

The others ate alone or in small groups at the picnic tables or back at their bunks. In addition to the families traveling together and the trio of teenagers, other units were beginning to form. Migrants from the same villages or states joined up and shared provisions and information with one another while people with similar destinations or objectives paired up or formed small groups. One of the women traveling alone started to take her meals with one of the unaccompanied men, and another young woman joined up with a family of four. Only the strong and the certain or the outcasts remained alone.

For the next two days, Job stayed up at night reading his Bible and slept until noon, when Ramon would arrive with food. Sometimes he ate with Cleary and sometimes he ate by himself. Because no one was working and no one had anywhere to go or anything to do, it was a place without time, and people slept and remained awake at all times. Each day, a few more people came until there were almost no beds left, and the stench of stale air and sweat became more and more difficult to bear.

Though he tried to keep to himself, Job couldn't help but hear the stories and discussions of the others. A young black couple from Arizona planned to find work in the solar panel factories in the fast-growing Xiong'an New Area of China, where immigrants were rumored to be welcome or at least tolerated. A Mexican American man sought kitchen work in a city and planned to bring over his family as soon as he could afford it. Two sisters whose father had died in an Arkansas mine collapse sought to make their way through China to Africa, where they heard there were even more opportunities in the growing areas of Lagos and Dar es Salaam and Konza Techno City. Job heard rumors about harrowing detention centers, immigration raids, and growing nationalist movements; there were stories about the gang rapes of migrant women, kidnapping and sex trafficking, and the firebombing of immigrant settlements. Others spoke about the ambivalence of the Chinese authorities and their encouragement of undocumented laborers, told by relatives already there who were enjoying a better quality of life than they'd had in the Americas. A middle-aged man who'd spent four years in the Zhongguancun Tech Zone before being deported back to California laughed and told them that all of their stories were rubbish, and after the young black woman started crying, her husband attacked the middle-aged man, and it took half a dozen people to pull them apart.

On the last day, seven more people arrived. Among them was an Indian American couple; the woman was six months pregnant and seemed nervous and reluctant, like a steer being corralled into a holding pen. Four of the others were men in their twenties and thirties and were traveling alone; a rumor began to swirl that one of them, who had a six-inch scar bisecting his face, had murdered a train guard up north. There was also an attractive young woman in her late teens whose ethnicity was impossible to tell—she could've been Hispanic, Native American, southeast Asian, African Caucasian, or some combination of those, or more. She wore black jeans and a tank top, and she had a purple birthmark on the right side of her neck that looked like a swallow's wing. Every man noticed her when she arrived and so did the women, too; she was impossible to ignore.

As the young woman looked for a bed, Cruze and his companions stared at her and made catcalls, but she ignored them. After a moment, Cruze noticed Job staring at her as well.

"The fuck you looking at, *pendejo*?" he said.

Job opened his mouth to reply, but before he could, Cruze had already walked away, and the others followed him, laughing. Job looked back at the young woman. When she glanced up in his direction and smiled, he felt a surge of electricity course through him as if he'd been struck by some sort of warm and gentle lightning.

It was still dark outside the warehouse when people began to stir. Many of the people staying there had been awake for hours or hadn't yet fallen asleep. There was a sense of nervousness and excitement and anticipation in the air like the feeling that precedes a fight or a first kiss or a summer storm; some talked in hushed tones or on cell phones, while others paced about or stared expectantly out grimy windows.

Job was already awake and had been awake for a few hours after finally surrendering to the fact that he wouldn't be able to sleep. For hours, he'd tossed and turned as he thought about the village he'd left and about what was waiting for him on the other side of the ocean. He envisioned looming towers and massive factories and other things he'd heard about or seen in pictures or on other people's tablets or phones. He thought about his mother, and he wondered if she still looked the same. Then he began to wonder if his memories of her were even accurate; the last time he'd seen her had been as a four-year-old—his memories were but vague snatches and glimpses—and he'd barely even recognized her in Eli's photo. Perhaps a sense or a feeling or just proximity might trigger something? What did he even remember about her, anyway? There was something about her voice, he recalled, something soothing and deep, like molasses. He remembered how strong her grip seemed, at least to him as a four-year-old, and the way she smelled vaguely of cloves and spice. But how could she remember him? He was no longer a toddler, and so much had changed since he was. Would she somehow be able to recognize her own offspring? Or would he be just another stranger to her in a vast sea of strangers?

He became more and more anxious and eventually just got up and read his Bible to try to clear his mind. He read some of the Proverbs, but he couldn't stop thinking about everything, so he skipped forward to the Book of Zechariah, where he found some distraction in the passage where the four horsemen came down from mountains of brass and went forward into the world. After he heard the steel door clang closed downstairs, he climbed down from the bunk bed and pulled on his shoes, glancing around at the others with him. He saw the husband of the pregnant woman sitting in a chair next to the bed where his wife slept. He saw Cleary sleeping beneath his twisted overcoat, with his back to the wall. He saw the attractive young woman reading from a small notebook. He saw Cruze and the other tattooed young men playing cards at one of the tables. He wondered what they were all leaving behind and where they were all going and what was waiting for them at their destinations. Even though he'd only known them for a few days and didn't really know any of them that deeply, he felt somehow already bound to them all as if they were part of some extended clan or some placeless village or perhaps survivors from the same shipwreck, although the shipwreck had yet to occur.

After a moment, Ramon finally reached their floor and entered the room. He was freshly showered and wore sunglasses and looked far more rested than they did.

"Grab your things," he said. "We leave in five minutes."

Those who were already up began or finished their packing. The others rose quickly and pulled on their clothing and gathered their possessions. A few minutes later, everyone funneled quietly down the stairwell carrying the entirety of their belongings in their backpacks and suitcases and bags. No one had that much. A change or two of clothing. A small family heirloom or item of value. Some necessary medication. Something to pass the time, or to prepare for what was to come. Some had nothing at all but the clothing on their backs and whatever items they carried in their pockets. A wallet. Currency. A pocketknife or a cell phone.

Once they reached the bottom of the stairwell, Ramon unlocked the rolling steel door and led them out into the predawn street, where an old tour bus awaited them. The side of the bus had a faded painting of a winged faerie over the words "TINKER BELL BUS LINES." A stocky man sucked at a vape pen as he stood by the open door of the bus, while another man stood by a luggage compartment and helped the people load their things before boarding.

Job got in line and filed onto the bus. There was an open aisle seat next to Cleary near the front, but he continued on and found a window seat near the back, next to the middle-aged man who'd spent four years in the Zhongguancun Tech Zone. He sat down, then watched as the young woman got aboard and found another window seat nearby.

Cruze and the others took the seats in the back, and the seats around them filled in until there weren't any left. There weren't enough seats for the children, so most of them sat on their parents' laps or squeezed in between them, and a few people stood in the aisle. As soon as everyone had boarded, the stocky man got on and sat down behind the wheel. Ramon got on after him and looked back and counted the passengers. After he finished, he turned and said something to the driver, and the driver started the engine and pulled away from the curb.

They picked up one of the city rings and took it toward the port. The roads were empty aside from an occasional delivery truck or eighteen-wheeler. When they arrived at the port, it was still dark outside. The myriad lights of the distant city-state of San Francisco kept the night sky from turning black the way it did back in the Willamette Valley and instead made it a dull purple the color of a light bruise.

The driver maneuvered the bus through a maze of shipping containers before pulling it into a hangar near the docks. As soon as the driver cut the engine, Ramon got off the bus and met a waiting group of men. Job watched as Ramon spoke to the leader of the group; the man had thick inky hair and the craggy, broken face of a pugilist, and judging by the way Ramon spoke to him, it was clear he was some sort of authority.

After talking to the man for a moment longer, Ramon returned to the bus.

"Let's go," he said.

The passengers grabbed their things and quickly filed off. Once they were outside, the men began to usher them toward the docks, where a number of speedboats awaited. As Job stepped off the bus, Ramon grabbed him and brought him over toward the leader of the group.

"This is Vargas," he said.

When Vargas saw Job, he looked back to Ramon.

"What the fuck is this?" he asked, speaking with the gravelly rasp of a lifelong smoker.

"This is your help," said Ramon.

"I told the Sister I needed another man, not a boy."

"Sorry, but he's all I got."

Vargas shook his head and walked off muttering toward the waiting speedboats, and Ramon pushed Job after him.

"Go on," said the young man. "Do what he says."

Job hurried after Vargas. Over at the docks, the other men were loading the passengers into the speedboats. Vargas shoved Job toward his men.

"Help them," he said.

Job assisted in loading the people onto the speedboats, and once they were all aboard, Vargas's men untied the mooring lines and fired up the speedboats' engines. From there, they left the port and headed out toward international waters.

As they rode out to sea, the passengers stood shoulder to shoulder in the tiny speedboats, tightly clutching their possessions or the boat's railings or each other. Some looked ahead for the vessel that would be taking them to China, and some looked back at the receding lights Oakland and of the walled city-state of San Francisco. Others looked at their feet or at the backs of those around them and tried not to get seasick as the speedboats bounced and slapped across the choppy waves. A few looked up where the stars still burned brightly in the sky; those who knew astrology could make out Andromeda's chains and the wings of the Pegasus and the Canes Venatici.

Before long, they were surrounded by darkness. There were no longer any lights behind them, and there were no lights in front of them, either. The only lights they could see were the lights of the other speedboats and the stars and the waxing moon in the sky overhead. The only sounds were of the engines and the slapping of the speedboats' hulls against the waves. The air was clean and bracing, and the sea spit a cold and salty mist in their faces every time the boats smacked down upon the crest of another wave.

Job closed his eyes and breathed in deep through his nose and smelled the air and tasted the salt water at the back of his throat. He'd never felt so unattached and free, and for a moment, he forgot about everything he'd been worrying about and fearing and felt like he was a bird, flying out over the water. After a while, he opened his eyes again and saw a few pinpoints of light appearing before them on the horizon. The lights grew larger and larger as they sped toward them until it became clear that they were the navigation lights of a tramp steamer. The whitewashed vessel was easily 120 feet long, if not longer, and had a thick chimney rising up from its center; a small Danish flag hung from its rear mast and the name *Hanne Pernille* was painted across the bow, and the closer they got to it, the more dilapidated and run-down the vessel appeared.

Job overheard one of the other passengers nearby.

"You've got to be kidding me," said the man.

Vargas's men cut the speedboats' engines and let the idling boats drift toward the ship. When they neared the ship, six men armed with machine guns approached the railing and tossed down rope ladders. Down in the speedboats, Job helped the men use boating poles to avoid crashing into the ship's hull.

Vargas turned and shouted to the passengers.

"Let's move, people!"

As some of the passengers began to climb the rope ladders, the man near Job turned to Vargas.

"I'm not going in that," he said.

"Then you can start swimming," said Vargas, climbing up one of the rope ladders without waiting for a reply.

One by one, the rest of the passengers followed him. One of the children traveling with her family piggybacked on her father as he climbed up; two young men held hands like small children, and the husband of the pregnant woman awkwardly pushed her up before him, shoving her swollen backside. As the waves rose and fell, some of the people slammed against the hull and struggled to hold on before continuing to ascend. One of the passengers dropped his satchel and the choppy black waves of the ocean quickly swallowed it; another fell into the water himself, and a couple of passengers screamed, but Vargas's men just seemed more annoyed than concerned. One threw the overboard man a life preserver while another fished him out of the water with a long boat hook.

After all of the passengers were finally aboard the vessel, Vargas counted them and then waved to the men in the speedboats. The men then swung the speedboats around in wide and lazy arcs and then fired the engines and began to head back toward land. As Job watched them go, Vargas turned back to address the passengers again.

"Welcome aboard," he said. "Until we get to China, you belong to me, so do whatever we tell you, and we'll try and make this as comfortable as possible."

Before anyone could reply, Vargas turned and nodded to his men, and the men began to usher the passengers toward a low door and then led them into a narrow stairwell leading down into the bowels of the ship. Job looked back to sea and watched the lights of the speedboats wink out in the distance and disappear before he followed the others. They funneled down the stairwell like cattle in slaughterhouse corrals, only able to see the backs of the heads and the feet of those in front of them. Once they finally got to the bottom of the stairwell, they entered a dark and musty twenty-five-by-forty-foot hold illuminated only by a few naked and grimy bulbs. The floors were covered with sawdust and straw, and the few small portholes were caked with scum. One of the passengers looked at the surroundings before turning back to Vargas's men.

"Where are we supposed to sleep?" he said.

"Wherever you want," said one of Vargas's men.

Once all the passengers were in the hold, Vargas's men climbed back up the stairs and then closed and locked the door behind them. Some of the passengers complained aloud to one another or under their breath, but the majority of them began carving out spaces for themselves and put down their bedrolls or began to make makeshift beds out of whatever they could and resigned themselves to the situation.

One of the small children began to cry.

"I want to go home," she said.

"We can't," said the child's mother. "Now hush."

Job found a dark and empty space in a corner of the hold. He kicked up some of the straw into a small pile and unrolled his blanket and spread it out onto the deck floor. He took off his boat shoes and put the things he'd been carrying inside the bedroll into one of the boat shoes and then put the boat shoes underneath the blanket and fashioned it into a makeshift pillow. Then he lay down and closed his eyes.

Even though he was exhausted, he was again far too anxious and excited to sleep. He thought more about his grandfather and about his brother and about his village. He thought more about China and what would be waiting there for him. He thought about his mother and he wondered how often she thought about him and if she ever even thought about him anymore. The thought suddenly occurred to him that she might not even be alive, but he quickly pushed it out of his mind and focused on other things. He thought about the ocean and about the things that lurked beneath the ship in its dark and endless waters; he could hear the creaking of the steamer's hull, and he could hear footsteps on the deck above them like muffled claps of far-off thunder. At some point just before dawn, he finally surrendered to his exhaustion and to the gentle rhythmic rocking of the boat and he fell asleep. In his sleep he dreamed he was back in the Cascades and it was early winter and he was heading up into the mountains. The sun was descending behind him and there was a spreading darkness on the horizon ahead of him, and the farther on he went, the darker it got until there was nothing at all until he heard muffled voices somewhere and then the voices became louder and closer and words began to form from the sounds, and then he woke and saw one of Vargas's men standing over him, cradling a scuffed machine gun.

"Get up."

Job quickly rose and emptied his shoes before pulling them on as he followed the man toward the stairwell leading up to the deck. Through one of the small portholes, he could see that it was light outside, though the sun wasn't yet up. At the top of the stairwell, the man rapped on the metal door and said something and then someone on the other side of the door unlocked a chain and opened the door. They went through and out onto the deck, and the man standing there closed the door and relocked the chain behind them.

The man with the machine gun, whose name was Draays, led Job through the galley, where three more men with machine guns sat at a table eating biscuits and canned stew and drinking coffee from dented steel mugs. Draays and Job continued on into the crew's quarters and passed a group of bunks with thin mattresses and then approached the door to a small bathroom.

"Get started on the shitter," said Draays, dropping a bucket at Job's feet and pointing toward the filthy toilet.

Job looked into the bowl. It was clogged with soiled tissue paper, brackish water, and human waste, and it looked like it had been that way for quite some time.

Job spent a couple hours scrubbing the toilets and sinks and then went up and mopped the deck. By the mast, one of Vargas's men switched the Danish flag with a South Korean one, and another man painted over the name of the ship on the hull.

Once he finished mopping, Job helped a fat man named Javier cook the crew a supper of canned chili and pasta. After serving it to them, he helped Javier cook some pots full of watery rice, and when the rice was ready, he took it in two big plastic buckets below decks to give to the passengers. They swarmed him when he came down the stairwell, and he couldn't dole out the food fast

101

enough. Some were thankful and gracious, and others were angry and jealous as if he was somehow an extension of their uncivilized chaperones. The attractive young woman, whose name he'd found out was Ynez, smiled at him as he gave her a portion; Cleary pleaded until he got some, and the husband of the pregnant woman gave his meager portion to his wife. Cruze and his friends shoved their way through the group and yanked the bucket from Job and served themselves heaping portions. Before Job could say anything, they shoved him to the floor and took their food back to their corner of the hold.

Job resumed serving the others and had to reduce the size of the portions, as there wasn't enough to go around. When he was finished serving them and they were finished eating, he took the buckets back above deck along with the buckets the passengers had used to relieve themselves. The contents stank worse than anything he'd ever smelled and splashed all over his legs as he carried them, and after he washed them and the crew's dishes, it was already dark and his fingers were raw and red. He returned back to the hold, where many of the passengers were already sleeping. He collapsed onto his bedroll and closed his eyes, and within minutes, he was soundly asleep.

They headed south for a few days and then turned and began to head west. As they went west, they avoided the major shipping lanes and stayed in between the North Pacific and North Equatorial currents. Without the trade winds at their backs, they occasionally lost speed or hit choppy stretches of ocean, but they avoided encountering anyone by traveling that way. Many countries already refused immigrant-filled vessels, and some even had a policy of firing upon them.

Job spent his days cleaning and preparing food and purifying salt water, and he spent his nights reading his Bible or watching some of the others in the hold play dominoes and mah jong with homemade game pieces fashioned from cardboard. Above deck, life was easy enough if not boring for the crew and they did whatever Vargas told them, and when there was nothing to do, which was much of the time, they also played card games and fished or drank beer and watched movies and television shows on tablets. Occasionally, Job would be asked to bring certain women above deck to the crew's quarters, but he wasn't told what it was for and he didn't ask, either; he assumed the women received some sort of compensation for what they were doing, or were somehow resigned to it, because none of them challenged it.

Below decks, life was harder, but it was not completely without amenities, and a rudimentary society began to develop among them much like it did in the country villages back home. The husband of the pregnant woman had been a nurse in San Francisco and looked after

103

their sick, while a man who had lived in China for four years before being deported taught basic language skills to anyone who was interested. A tailor who had brought along a few needles was able to mend clothes, and one of the young women gave massages for extra water or rice or whatever she could get. Others found more solitary pursuits to pass the time; one man whittled scraps of wood into chess pieces, and another read a dog-eared Koran and prayed five times a day toward Mecca using a watch and a tiny compass to guide him.

Though he didn't seek it out, Job himself found a place in the emerging society as well as becoming an intermediary between the crew and the passengers. They asked him to pass along requests to Vargas for things like more food or the use of the restroom upstairs or the chance to go above deck for part of the day, and Vargas in turn sent updates or commands through him. Serving two opposed masters was a difficult and frustrating position to be in, but he found it easier to do if he just delivered the messages and kept as detached and impartial as possible.

By the time they'd passed Hawaii, they'd been at sea for two weeks. Job's face and neck and arms were corded with muscle and browned from working under the sun, while many of those in the hold were paler and thinner than they'd been at the beginning of the journey. They'd been fortunate with the weather and had avoided any storms other than an occasional rain, but the increasingly squalid conditions of the hold coupled with the dwindling supplies caused enough unrest among the passengers that Vargas finally gave in to some of their requests and allowed them to go above deck for an hour each day to exercise or use the restroom or fish with improvised rods under the supervision of the armed men.

One afternoon during the hours the passengers were allowed above deck, Draays sent Job to the storage room to get batteries. When Job unlocked the door, he found Ynez inside, sitting on some sacks of rice and reading a tattered book.

"What are you doing here?" he said, startled.

"Studying," she replied, holding up the book, which had Chinese symbols on it.

He hesitated, the words getting lost somewhere between his brain and mouth.

"You're not gonna tell on me, are you?" she asked.

He hesitated again for a moment and then quickly shook his head. She smiled, and he smiled back. The quarters were so close that he could smell her; she had a sharp and spicy scent that appealed to some primal part of him, and for a moment, he forgot why he was there.

"You gonna leave the door open all day?" she asked.

Remembering what he'd come for, he looked into one of the boxes on the shelves and took out a package.

"Batteries," he said, stating the obvious and immediately regretting it.

She smiled again before looking back to her book. Embarrassed, he turned and made his way to the door. He stopped there and hesitated again for a moment then turned and looked back to her.

"How do you say good-bye?" he asked.

"What?"

"In Chinese," he said, nodding to the book. "How do you say good-bye?"

"*Zài jiàn.*"

"Well," he said. "*Zài jiàn.*"

She shook her head but couldn't help but smile, then resumed studying. He left the room, closing and locking the door behind him.

Out in the hallway, his heart pounded in his chest like a bird trying to break free from a cage.

They continued west. At some point, they crossed the international date line, but none of them were keeping track anymore or knew what day of the week it was much less what hour, so the crossing mattered little. Of those who had watches, most had already taken them off and put them away, and of those who were still wearing them, they were wearing them merely out of habit rather than for timekeeping. Even the Muslim had to guess when it was that they passed over the antipodes of the Kaaba and when he should change from facing east when praying to facing west; the lines and boundaries of man were even more abstract and meaningless when there were no landmasses or solid ground to fix them to.

They were blessed with favorable weather aside from a squall they encountered just north of Micronesia. Job was above deck when the shelf cloud first appeared on the horizon, and he hustled about the ship with the rest of the crew as they tried to outrun the storm. The massive gray wall kept rolling toward them until it was so close that they could see its ragged and wind-torn undersides just above them, but before the storm overtook them, its winds shifted direction and they pulled free from its grip. They escaped it with only a day of heavy rains and later watched as a rainbow materialized behind them in its wake.

Job continued to do whatever Vargas and his crew asked of him and continued to serve as the voice of the passengers in the hold whenever issues arose. When he wasn't being badgered by the passengers or bossed around by the crew, he preferred to keep to himself. He came upon Ynez in the storage room a few more times, and each time he did, he learned a few new Chinese words from her, and he learned something personal about her each time as well. He learned that she'd grown up in Oakland with her *abuela* and had never met her own parents. He learned she'd gone to school for a while and had excelled at math and science, but she didn't have the connections nor the money to study further. He learned that she'd worked in a factory making crayons but hated it and was going to China in hopes of studying engineering there. He also learned that she had a fiancé, Daniel, who was already there in Shanghai, awaiting her. She was confident yet modest, and every time he asked her something, she'd answer succinctly and turn the focus to him. She asked him where he was from, and where he was going, and what he wanted to do. He thought his own story and plans were far less interesting than hers and told her so, but she shook her head and smiled and told him there was so much more to his story than that.

At nights, he often lay awake thinking of his mother. More and more, he found himself thinking of Ynez as well. He'd never been around someone who'd made him feel so special, and her optimism was contagious. He'd lie there in the sweltering dark of the hold and listen to the soft slapping of the waves against the hull and watch the curves of her back and her side while she slept and trace the geometry of her body with his eyes, as if in the study and memorization of her features might be hidden some secret pathway to her heart. He'd rehearse things he wanted to say to her and things he wanted to ask her and by the imagining of her responses he'd reforge and whittle back his lines like some playwright honing his work, but every time he encountered her, the words would get lost somewhere between his head and his lips and he'd end up having nothing to say, or worse yet, he'd say awkward or juvenile things. She never made him feel bad about it, though; on the contrary, she somehow seemed to halve his uneasiness and let him know that it was not only all right to stumble, but that it was somehow normal and human.

While cleaning above deck one day, he found some dog-eared magazines lying in the crew's quarters; they were filled with photographs of celebrities and athletes and expensive watches and cars, and they were written in Chinese. He waited until the crew left and then he took the magazines and hid them underneath his shirt and brought them below decks to give to Ynez, but she wasn't there, so he left them for her beneath her blanket. When he finished putting them there, he saw that Cleary was watching him. From the look on Cleary's face, he couldn't tell whether Cleary was jealous or felt sorry for him, or perhaps both. The next time he encountered Ynez in the storage room, she thanked him for the magazines.

"You didn't have to do that," she said.

"I know," he replied, grinning and finally not trying to think of the right thing to say.

She taught him a few helpful verbs—to want, to take, to be, to have—and some important phrases, like thank you, you're welcome, how much, and I don't understand. He couldn't pull his gaze away from her, and before long, she noticed it again, but this time, she said nothing and simply gazed back at him. Maybe it was the proximity, or the sweltering heat, or all the days at sea, or all of those things and other things as well, but time seemed to stop for a moment and they got lost in each other's eyes. After a long, long moment, he leaned forward and kissed her, and she let him, even kissing him back for a moment before catching herself and pulling away.

"I can't," she said, getting up.

"Wait," he said, getting up after her.

Ynez squeezed into a passageway that led back down into the hold. Job went to follow her, but before he could, he heard Draays shout for him out in the hallway.

He didn't see Ynez for the next few days. He spent much of his time working above deck, and the few times he was below, it was usually too late or too early and too dark to look for her.

He stole away from his duties as often as he could to check the storage room, but after the day he'd kissed her, he didn't see her there again. After a few days, he stopped looking; it was clear she was avoiding him, not even lining up for food whenever he'd dole it out. He spent more and more time above deck, focusing on his duties and trying not to think of her. He refilled empty plastic milk jugs with purified seawater, cleaned out the plastic buckets they used for toilets below decks, cleaned the bathrooms above deck, and helped Javier prepare food for the crew.

One morning, Javier sent him to the storage room to get more salt. He didn't even think about Ynez, having given up on seeing her in there again. When he unlocked the door to the storage room, though, he saw her, being held down by Cruze's friends. Her eyes were as wide as saucers, and she was fighting them like a hog-tied animal.

Cruze turned around from struggling to pull down her jeans and saw Job.

"Walk away, boy," he said.

Job didn't move.

"You deaf?" said Cruze. "I said walk away."

"Let her go."

Cruze turned to the others, and one of the other young men lunged for Job, but Job sidestepped him and hit him on the side of the temple, and the young man went down. Ynez pulled free from Cruze and attacked his other friend, screaming; Cruze rushed Job, and Job moved to sidestep him, too, but Cruze tackled him at the waist. They went crashing to the deck in a heap, where Cruze began pummeling him, and the other young man joined in.

Job covered up to defend himself, but Cruze and the other young man throttled him. Ynez ran out into the hallway, shouting for help. Job held his hands to his face and weathered the barrage as best as he could, and when Cruze finally paused for breath, Job drove his knee into Cruze's groin. Cruze rolled off him, sucking for air, and as Job scrambled to his feet, the one he'd knocked down tackled him before he could leave the room. They slammed to the deck, and Cruze staggered over and kicked Job in the stomach, and then the face. The pain was unbelievable, but Job kept struggling to pull free from the young men as they kicked him again and again.

Just before he passed out, Job saw Draays approach and smash Cruze in the face with the butt of his rifle.

When he finally opened his eyes, Job didn't recognize where he was. At first, he thought he might've died, but when he saw the other bunks and felt the rolling of the waves beneath him, he realized he was in the crew's quarters. His head was ringing and his whole body felt like it was on fire; some of his teeth felt loose, and his mouth was as dry as sand. Through the portholes, he could see that it was night. He tried to get up, but he couldn't, so instead, he just opened his mouth and groaned. Someone in the galley heard him and said something to someone else, and a moment later, Javier waddled into the crew's quarters with a soggy and unlit cigar clamped in his teeth.

"How long have I been out?" asked Job.

"Three days," said Javier. "We didn't think you'd make it."

"I need to get up—"

Job nearly fell out of bed, but Javier stopped him.

"Easy," he said.

Javier shouted toward the next room, and Draays entered from the galley with a plastic jug. He gave it to Job, and Job drank greedily.

"Not so fast," said Javier.

Job gagged on the water and spit some back up and then drank some more. It burned as it went past his ribs. When he was finished drinking, Javier took the bottle back from him and Job lay back down on the bed and closed his eyes and almost immediately fell back asleep. The next

112

time he opened his eyes, he was startled to see sun coming in through the portholes and Vargas sitting in a chair across from him. For a moment, he thought he might be dreaming until he smelled the bucket of feces next to the bed.

"You're an idiot, you know that?" said Vargas.

Job tried to struggle to his feet, but Vargas stopped him.

"Don't," said Vargas.

"I can work—"

"I'll get what you owe me later," said Vargas. "Just rest for now. You're not worth anything to me dead."

Job spent two more days recuperating in the crew's quarters. He spent his time looking at magazines and staring out at the open sea and playing solitaire with a deck of cards missing the eight of spades. At night, he ate whatever soft foods he could handle with the crew and listened to their stories about running guns in Bangladesh and Somalia and transporting migrants from Northern Africa up to Italy and Spain, before Europe collapsed. He almost forgot his reason for being aboard the ship, but then he would see Javier or someone else lugging a bucket of rice down to the hold, and he'd begin to feel guilty for being above deck.

The following morning, Job finally left the crew's quarters. The conditions in the hold were still uncomfortable, and things were even filthier than before. Fetid buckets of waste serving as makeshift toilets stood in corners; laundry done in dirty water hung drying from the rafters, and the sawdust and straw on the floor had become moldy and brown. As he glanced around, he noticed that Cruze and his two friends were no longer among the passengers. When he asked Cleary about it, Cleary said he didn't know. Someone else told him they were being kept in a storage room.

Job went over to the spot where he'd left his bedroll and found his things exactly as he'd left them. As he lay on the bedroll, he felt something underneath his back. He moved aside the bedroll and found the pages of his Bible with some folded sheets of paper inside them. He took them out and looked them over, immediately recognizing Ynez's handwriting; there were dozens of phrases written in English with their Pinyin and traditional translations next to them. Phrases like, *HELLO. HOW ARE YOU? DO YOU SPEAK ENGLISH? HOW MUCH DOES THAT COST?*

There was also a note at the bottom of the last page that said, *GET TO KNOW THESE IF YOU CAN . . . THEY'LL HELP YOU MORE THAN ANYTHING IN THAT BIBLE WILL.*

Job resumed his duties. He helped Javier cook and he cleaned the toilets and he swabbed the decks. Though it hurt to raise his arms, he said nothing; he wanted to do something. The time went faster when he was busy, and the stench of sweat and mold and urine in the hold was unbearable. He preferred to be above deck with the sun and the wind and the sea despite whatever pain it entailed.

He eventually saw Ynez again, but too much time had passed to bring up the kiss, so it remained unspoken. He felt an awkwardness around her, and she seemed to feel the same around him, so they avoided each other. As the ship passed the Mariana Islands, one of the older men traveling alone whose health had deteriorated started to complain about chest pains and turned ashen. Before they could figure out what to do for him, he went into cardiac arrest. They carried him above deck and tried to revive him there, but they couldn't get his heart beating again. He died with his mouth screwed up into a twisted grimace and his pants soaked with urine. Before the body was even cold, the man who'd spent four years in the Zhongguancun Tech Zone took his boots and another claimed his belt and jacket and then a number of others descended upon him and his remaining possessions like vultures until he had nothing on him but a pair of tattered underwear and two mismatched socks.

Javier and Draays wrapped the man's corpse in a burlap sack and then tied it up with rope. Vargas asked if anyone wanted to say anything, but no one knew anything about the man, other than that he'd had experience welding, fought in the Northern African wars, and had come from New San Antonio, so they weighed down the corpse with a cinder block and dropped it over the side. As Job watched the body sink below the waves, he felt a chill run through his body. He couldn't imagine a fate worse than being jettisoned overboard like trash to spend eternity in that vast nothingness, fixed to nothing and nowhere in particular.

They steamed their way past the Philippine Sea. As they approached the Ryukyu Islands, they were nearly out of provisions and only had enough for a ladleful of watery rice and a few sips of desalinized water per person per day. The passengers grew dehydrated and constipated, and some of them developed bleeding gums and jaundiced skin. Despite finally beginning to approach their destination land, rather than becoming relieved, they seemed to grow more and more panicked the closer they got.

After they entered the East China Sea, the pregnant woman woke up in the middle of the night in labor. Knowing they were only a day or two from the coast, her husband tried to prevent it by giving her a warm bath up in the crew's quarters, hoping it might forestall the child's coming. It appeared at first as if it was going to work and that it might pass until they reached land, but then in the hours just before dawn, her contractions returned and became longer in duration, and she soon began going into labor.

Just after the sun came up behind them, the woman delivered a five-and-a-half-pound baby girl. The child came prematurely into the world, dark purple and slicked with vernix and blood, and she had a full head of thick black hair. Despite being undersized, she cried louder than any of them expected. Had the ship been official, they would have taken note of the latitude and longitude and marked it down in the log, but as it was an illegal vessel full of illegal passengers, she became a child of no country with no citizenship, born on no fixed land to call her home. She was from everywhere yet nowhere, and though her parents had chosen another name for her before they'd begun the journey, they decided to call her Mare instead since she'd arrived at sea.

Job took the bucket that contained the afterbirth and placenta above deck and dumped it overboard and watched it swirl and turn over and sink in the curling eddies of their wake. He again felt the chill he'd felt when they dumped the corpse, as if he was beginning to understand that he, too, like everything else, was perhaps destined to return to some infinite void, and that unlike the bright and warm and divine light he grew up hearing his grandfather describe, it might actually be dark and empty and of this world.

Vargas approached on his way toward the pilothouse and saw the vernix-stained bucket in Job's hands, and he couldn't help but shake his head.

"It's amazing how stupid people are," he said. "They can't even take care of themselves, yet they choose to bring others into the world."

Job said nothing. They stood there, staring toward the horizon. After a moment, Vargas broke the silence.

"You got any plans for when we arrive?" he asked.

Job nodded.

"Find my mother," he said.

"You mean you don't know where she is?"

"She was in Guangzhou."

"When was that?"

"Ten years ago."

"I've got work for you if you want it," said Vargas. "I was standing right about where you are about forty years ago, on a barge from Portugal to Africa. Just like you and every other asshole below deck, and below every deck of every other ship steaming toward China and Africa right now. The day I stopped chasing dreams and started selling them was the day I started living."

"That's all right," said Job.

Vargas pursed his lips and shook his head but said nothing. After a long moment, he turned and continued his way up toward the pilothouse.

The following night, a few hours after the passengers had gone to sleep, the door leading into the hold opened and Draays shouted down.

"Everybody up!"

The passengers quickly rose and gathered their things. Then they filed up the stairwell. Once above deck, they saw Vargas and his men, and they could see a number of fishing boats bobbing in the choppy waters below.

As the fishing boats approached, they could see armed men aboard each one.

"Let's move out," said Vargas.

The fishing boats drew close to the tramp steamer, and Vargas and his men herded the passengers toward the side of the ship. As one of the fishing boats began to rise upon a cresting wave and the tramp steamer began to dip upon a falling one, Vargas timed it and pushed one the passengers off the steamer and onto the deck of the fishing boat. The men aboard the fishing boat caught the passenger and pushed him back and out of the way.

"Let's go, people," said Vargas. "Move."

One by one, the passengers on the tramp steamer waited for the vessel to drop enough so they could time their jumps over onto to the smaller boats. Some of them timed it perfectly and practically stepped from one deck onto the other; others came up short and crashed to the decks of the fishing boats or caught the railings and hung there, trying to avoid being crushed as the vessels collided. One unlucky passenger got his leg smashed between the steamer and one of the fishing boats, and he fell screaming into the choppy black waters. When some of the men on one of the fishing boats pulled him to safety, those who were still on the tramp steamer could see his left foot dangling and pointing inward at an impossible angle.

"Keep moving," shouted Vargas.

They continued to off-load the passengers. The children of the families shook their heads and cried until Vargas's men wrested them free from their parents and tossed them over to those who were waiting below. The woman with the baby also refused to go, but her husband took the bundled baby from her and cradled it in his arms and jumped, and once he landed, she jumped after him and grimaced as she came down and promptly took back her baby. Ynez perfectly timed her jump and practically stepped onto the deck of one of the fishing boats; Job went after her just as seamlessly. When Cleary jumped over, he missed the boat he was aiming for and belly flopped into the choppy water with a loud slap. He came up thrashing and gasping for air until they threw him a life preserver with a rope tethered to it. Then they pulled him close enough to fish him out with a pole.

Vargas shoved Cruze and his two friends onto the last waiting boat before following them aboard. Once safely on deck with them, he counted those around him and got head counts from the other three boats as well. When he finished counting, he raised a finger and made a small circular motion in the air, and the men on the fishing boats turned them around and headed back in the direction from which they'd came. As the engines groaned to life, Job glanced back at the tramp steamer behind them; within seconds, it was little more than a pair of lights on the horizon, and a moment after that, it was gone.

They rode toward the coast standing shoulder to shoulder on the cramped decks of the fishing boats. The engines were too loud to talk over, but even if they hadn't been, it was unlikely that anyone would've wanted to talk. They were all too excited to be finally reaching land, and they all had their eyes fixed on the horizon ahead of them. After a while, a few interspersed lights began to appear along the coastline, materializing in the darkness like the first stars of night. The passengers stood on their toes and arched or leaned over the railings to see them. As they continued on, more and more lights appeared; great glowing cities cropped up and towering buildings appeared out of thin air. The sky became lilac-colored from all the light pollution, and there were endless strings of lights as far as the eye could see.

Job glanced around for Ynez. After a moment, he spotted her near the bow of one of the fishing boats, next to another young woman traveling alone. Ynez was the only one on board who didn't look excited.

If anything, she looked afraid.

Anyone who ever had a dog knows they can sense things. When I was a boy, we used to have this little pit mix we found by the river. This was before meat got so scarce that people stopped having dogs as pets and started eating them. We called him Jelly. He was smart as a whip. He could sense storms coming from almost half a day away. There wouldn't even be a cloud in the sky and he'd start moaning. It was the strangest thing. He'd whine real low and drawn out like he was singing a sad song. Then five or six hours later, the black clouds would come along, and with them, a storm. He could sense fear in people, too. And other things. Like bad intentions. This one time a stranger came into our village, a real pretty lady with hair as black as coal. She had lots of beans with her and some strange sort of meat. She was looking to sell it or get something in trade. She was awful friendly, but Jelly wasn't having any of it. He wouldn't let her get within ten feet of me or Eli. Kept barking like all get-out. She tried trading with a couple of others and then finally just left and then a few days later some guys from one of the villages upriver showed up looking for her. Turns out she'd killed one of their group and took everything he had. Even cut off one of his legs, which was probably that strange-looking meat she had. And it's not just dogs, either. I've heard stories of other animals sensing things. There was a flood by the coast a few years before I was born and one of the old-timers said that just before it happened, the animals started heading toward higher ground. Cats and bears and squirrels and everything just up and ran and got as high up in the trees as they could in the middle of a bright sunny day. He even saw a black bear clinging to a treetop and practically tipping it over. The deer and rabbits and everything else that couldn't climb just went up into the hills and the old-timer said that he figured he should maybe do the same, and then an hour later, a big black wave came along and washed everything away and most of the houses and people along with it. We could probably sense things more, too, if we didn't have so much else going on to distract us. Cloud patterns. Magnetic fields. Air pressure. Things that don't have names or haven't even been figured out yet or quantified or defined. I've experienced a bit of it myself when I've been out hunting for a few days, when I'm just studying the wind and what's on it and the tracks in the earth. Not talking or thinking but just being present and in the moment. There's plenty to be seen if you're open and ready for it. The only problem is that we just usually aren't.

When I first set foot on solid ground in China, I figured I would get a sense about it. Something good or something bad or even something mixed. But I didn't get anything.

Maybe that was something, though.

III

The fishing boats turned and went north along the rocky
coast toward an undeveloped area. The farther they went,
the fewer lights there were and the darker the night sky
became. They eventually neared some docks, where a
group of armed men waited in the darkness. Job could
make them out by the glowing ends of their cigarettes and
by the reflections the moonlight made on their rifle
barrels. As the boats approached the docks, the crews
threw lines to the men, who quickly tied up the boats and
began helping the passengers disembark.

The armed men led Vargas and the others toward a
trio of moving trucks. As soon as Job stepped off the docks
and onto land, his knees buckled, and he stumbled and
nearly fell. It felt strange being on solid ground after being

at sea for so long. While he went forward, he glanced around at his surroundings; although it was dark, he could make out a number of trees and shrubs, yellow-green sand sedges and dark bindweed and other plants he'd never seen back home. He could also see a vague outline of the Leizhou Peninsula to the south and the craggy volcanoes that dotted its low-lying plains like stubble.

Once they reached the moving trucks, the armed men corralled the passengers into the trailers. Then they rolled down the metal doors of the trucks and locked them into place. Everything went black, and something about it reminded Job of the cattle cars he and Eli used to see going past on the train tracks that cut through the Willamette valley. A sick and uneasy feeling grew in the pit of his stomach.

They sat there and waited in the cold darkness. One by one, they heard the engines outside rumble to life. Then their truck lurched forward and drove off. They rode jostling into one another along some windy and slow sections of road and then picked up a long stretch that seemed straight. Judging by their speed, Job assumed they were on some sort of highway.

They rode for what felt like a great distance. As they traveled, Job heard snippets of hushed conversations around him. Worried children expressing their fears to their parents. Guesses at where they were being taken, and stories they'd heard from the ones who'd gone before them and wrote back about it.

After a few hours, they slowed and began turning often and occasionally stopping and then starting again. Outside, there were noises of a city. Car horns. Motorcycles and mopeds. An occasional siren. At one point when they stopped, Job thought he could hear people talking outside, though he couldn't make out what language they were speaking. At another point, he heard what sounded like a barking dog, and then he heard what may have been fireworks.

The truck eventually pulled to a stop and the engine shut off. Job and the others sat in the darkness like excited audience members waiting for the curtain to rise. They soon heard doors opening and boots hitting the ground, and then they heard approaching footsteps and padlocks being unlocked. Then the roll door went clattering up, and as light flooded into the trailer, Job and the others squinted out at the inside of a vast and brightly lit warehouse. There were no windows, and it was impossible to tell whether it was day or night.

"Welcome to China," said Draays.

Those who'd already paid for their passage were allowed to leave as soon as they arrived at the warehouse. The others were brought to a damp and musty holding area where they waited, locked up as if chattel, for family or

friends to bring the balances of what they owed or they
made arrangements with loan sharks and factory owners
who were looking for workers.

When he got to the holding area, Job glanced around
for Ynez. They'd traveled in separate trucks, and he hadn't
seen her since they'd arrived at the warehouse. Before he
could find her, Draays approached him with a burly
Chinese man in a hooded jacket. The man had a faded
tattoo of a Chinese symbol curling across one side of his
neck.

"This is Zhou," said Draays. "You'll be working for
him at a factory in Dongguan."

Zhou said something in Chinese to Draays, and
Draays replied to him in Chinese before turning back to
Job.

"Good luck," he said.

Before Job could reply, Zhou yanked him by the
collar and shoved him toward the back of a fourteen-foot
box truck parked nearby. A number of the passengers
from the steamer were already getting into it, and he
recognized a family of four from the steamer and two of
the women who'd been traveling alone.

Job glanced around the warehouse one more time for
Ynez, but he couldn't find her. He began to feel an
emptiness he hadn't felt since Eli's death, and then began
to feel guilty for thinking about her rather than his
brother. She was just a stranger, he thought to himself, but
Eli was family. Then he watched as one of the passengers

bolted toward an exit. Two of Zhou's men caught up to the passenger before he could get there and tackled him to the floor, then pummeled him senseless.

Zhou shoved Job into the back of the truck with the others, and Job found an open space and sat on the floor with his bedroll in his lap. After another man from the steamer who was also traveling alone got in, Zhou rolled down the roll door behind them and locked it.

Everything went black again, and Job felt like he was at the bottom of a deep well.

They rode for another hour. At first, they were moving fast, and Job assumed they were on a highway again. At some point, they began moving slower and there was a lot of stopping and starting, which Job imagined was due to traffic. The truck eventually stopped, and they heard a gate being unlocked outside; the truck then went forward a bit and then stopped again, and the engine shut off and they heard the driver's-side door open. After a moment, they heard footsteps approaching the back of the truck and then heard a padlock being unlocked and the roll door went up, and they saw Zhou and a pair of Chinese men with broad shoulders and scarred faces. Outside, the sun was down and the world had taken on the hue of tarnished silver.

"Everybody out," said Zhou. "*Xiànzài.*"

The people got out of the truck and followed Zhou and his men toward a loading bay outside another warehouse. As Zhou unlocked a door, Job looked back and noticed a chain link fence topped with concertina wire surrounding the warehouse. He got another sick feeling in his stomach, but before he could say anything, they were ushered inside.

After they were all in the warehouse, one of Zhou's men locked the door behind them and led them to a windowless room in the basement. The room was dimly lit by two overhead fluorescent tubes, and there were two dozen people already there sitting on mats or lying on sleeping bags and bedrolls. In one corner of the room lay a pile of stained and ratty sleeping bags; a duct-taped kerosene space heater stood in another corner of the room. Some of the walls had photographs or pictures or prayer cards taped to them. A pair of creased leather shoes was next to one unrolled sleeping bag, while a fraying towel hung from a hook on the wall near another pile of blankets. It smelled like sweat and kerosene and mold. Zhou's man pointed to the unoccupied sleeping bags.

"Sleep in here," he said, ripping a bunch of photos off the wall. "Breakfast is at seven and you work at eight."

"When do we go out?" asked one of the men.

Zhou's man laughed.

"You don't," he said, and without waiting for a reply, he left the room, locking the door behind him.

The new arrivals went forward and began staking out places to sleep. The family of four spread out a group of sleeping bags near each other. Job approached the far corner of the room and began unpacking his things next to a bunched-up sleeping bag. The others found unattended bedrolls or mats and began unloading their things and setting up their makeshift beds.

Job took off his shoes and placed them at the end of his bedroll. Then he lay down with the bunched-up sleeping bag under his head. Looking up, he noticed a photograph taped to the wall that Zhou's man forgot to take down, of a woman and a young boy that looked like it'd been taken somewhere in America. The woman wasn't much older than Job and seemed like she was too young to be a mother. She had stringy hair and a crude tattoo of a cartoon bird on her right shoulder, and there was something sad about the way she smiled. In the photograph, she was reaching down to hold the boy's hand. The grinning boy was struggling to stand up on his own on his reedy legs like a newborn foal, beaming with pride.

Job closed his eyes. As he lay there, he couldn't help but wonder about the person who'd left the photograph behind. Had it belonged to the woman in the photograph, or someone close to her? He wondered if the people in the photograph were together, then began to wonder why the person had left the photograph behind and if something had happened to the person. The more he thought about it, the more uneasy he became. He finally just took down the photograph and slid it underneath someone else's bedroll, then closed his eyes and tried to sleep, but he couldn't no matter what he tried.

The image of the woman and her boy lingered in his mind like a sunspot.

Sometime before dawn, Job finally fell asleep. In his dreams, he was still at sea, and he was working below decks bailing water. He was making no headway, though, and the faster he bailed, the faster the water rose. It started at his ankles and rose to his knees and was soon past his waist and approaching his chest. When the lights in the dorm came on, he woke up, gasping for air.

"Wake up," said one of Zhou's men.

Job glanced around at his surroundings and saw most of the others crawling out from their sleeping bags and bedrolls and stretching and rising and wiping the sleep from their eyes. He got up as well and began to pull on his shoes. As he did so, another one of Zhou's men tossed a garbage bag full of stale rolls into the center of the room. The people rushed toward the garbage bag and began to snatch up the bread. As was the case on the steamer, those who got to it first got the most, and those who got to it last got the least and the stalest. Job got there late and didn't get anything at all save for some stony crusts, but an older boy who'd gotten three rolls saw that Job was empty-handed and offered him one of his.

Job hesitated, distrustful.

"Go on," said the boy. "You're gonna need it."

The boy offered again, and seeing no malice in the boy's eyes, Job took the roll.

"Thanks," he said.

"You're from Oregon, aren't you?"

Job hesitated again, suspicious.

"I can hear it in your voice," said the boy. "Most whites who come through here are from the West Coast."

"I'm from Ellendale," said Job.

"Valsetz. My name's Ethan."

"I'm Job."

They shook hands.

"How long you been here?" asked Job.

"Six months," said Ethan. "I'd say it gets better, but it don't."

After the workers finished eating, they followed Zhou's men into the hallway and up a stairwell and into a large and cluttered room full of makeshift workstations. Some of the workstations had ramshackle and mismatched sewing machines and equipment on them, while others had dangerous-looking jigsaws or infrared ovens or worn machine presses.

Job looked around at the shoddy equipment, surprised.

"I thought all the factories over here were high-tech?"

Ethan laughed.

"Not the ones where we work," he said.

Zhou's men looked over the new workers. They assigned the women to the stitchers at the sewing machines and the men to the assemblers at the machine presses. The children were assigned to the finishers at the end of the line, and Job was assigned to the group of cutters.

One of Zhou's men turned to some of the older workers.

"Show them what to do," he said. "*Kuài kuài.*"

The new workers joined their groups and watched as the experienced workers demonstrated the various tasks. Job watched as the cutters stamped sheets of mesh fabric into curved pieces, crescent moons and kidneys and fat banana shapes. Farther down the line, he could see a group of stitchers sewing the pieces together and then passing them on to the sole workers, who used the infrared ovens to glue the soles together. Beyond them were the assemblers, who stretched the shoe uppers over a mold and glued the uppers and the soles together using large machine presses. At the end of the line were the finishers, who checked the completed shoes for flaws before boxing them. The process was industrial and orderly though it seemed recklessly fast, and the hands of the workers were calloused and scarred. Most of the stitchers' fingernails were mottled like oyster shells, and the fingertips of the sole workers were blistered and scabbed over.

Within minutes of being there, Job was tasked to help feed uncut sheets of mesh fabric into one of the stamp presses. As soon as he loaded them, another man lowered the press and it sliced the mesh to pieces. Then a third man removed the cut pieces from the press and pushed them along down the line. The clanging din of the machines was too loud to talk over and it was hard to even think above the noise. In order to keep up, they had to work fast, and Job had to time it just right or the press would come down on his hands like a guillotine. A few times it got close, and before long, he was sweating in order to keep pace.

The morning went by quickly, and at noon they ate a cold lunch of watery congee and more stale rolls. The food was bland and mostly carbohydrates, but Job was glad to have it. After lunch, they resumed work. During the afternoon, one of the workers at Job's station incorrectly loaded a piece of mesh, and as he reached back in to move it, the man working the press didn't see him and lowered the press onto the man's hand. It sliced off two of the man's fingers at the knuckles, and two hot strings of blood rose snakelike from the tiny stumps and splashed the machine in front of him. The man screamed and pulled his hand to his chest, and they stopped the line for a moment. Someone rushed toward the man with a dirty towel; someone else picked up the man's severed digits and wrapped them in a piece of fabric and gave them to one of Zhou's men as two others helped lead the man away.

135

Another one of Zhou's men assigned one of the finishers to take the injured man's place, and an older woman wiped down the machine with some more rags. Within minutes of it happening, all traces of the accident were gone and they had resumed working.

At four o'clock, they stopped for dinner and then resumed working again. At ten, one of Zhou's men barked an order, and the machines stopped. Then the tired workers trudged quietly back to their subterranean quarters. When they got back to their room in the basement, Job grabbed his towel and made his way toward the bathroom. After waiting forty-five minutes, it was finally his turn, and he went in and washed his hands and face and brushed his teeth with his finger. There was no hot water left, and there was hardly any water pressure at all.

He made his way back toward their quarters after he finished, and when he got there, the people were talking quietly in small groups or reading or playing cards or checkers on handmade boards. Others ate pieces of stale bread they'd squirreled away or dried nuts or fruit or other things they'd traded for with Zhou's men. In one corner, a mother was reading a tattered picture book to a child, and in another corner someone else was studying Chinese. Many of the others were already asleep.

Job hung up his towel on a nail. Then he took off his shoes and put them at the end of his bedroll. He thought about taking out his Bible to read or studying the phrases

Ynez had given him, but he was exhausted. Instead, he just lay down and closed his eyes. Within moments, he was asleep, and in his sleep, he had no dreams, and it felt like no time had passed at all when one of Zhou's men came and woke them the following morning.

The second day at the factory was exactly the same as the first. They rose at seven o'clock, were on the line by eight, stopped briefly for lunch and dinner, and finished at ten. The work was exhausting and monotonous, but the ever-present possibility of injury kept Job focused and alert. When the day was over, he was too tired to do anything but sleep, and as soon as he closed his eyes, he was out, and the next thing he knew one of Zhou's men was waking them again.

By the end of the week, his hands were calloused and his back ached, but he was glad he still had all his fingers. One of the other new workers lost a pinky when a machine press flattened it; another sliced off the tips of his middle and ring fingers with a jigsaw. Someone was injured nearly every day.

After two weeks, they were given a Sunday off; no one came to wake them in the morning, and Job slept until noon. He watched television with some of the others and played checkers with Ethan, and before he knew it, it was nighttime again and he went to sleep.

At seven o'clock the following morning, one of Zhou's men came to wake them, and by eight they were back on the line again. The days piled up into weeks and the weeks soon became months. Though the work was grueling, the fact there was so much of it made the time go by faster. Every day he spent on the line, Job believed he was one day closer to leaving the factory and one day closer to being able to look for his mother. Though they were welcome respites, the rare days off were more difficult than the days working because they went by slower, and there was more time for him to think.

The muscles in Job's arms became more defined over time, and he grew another inch and his pants became too small for him. As he became accustomed to the workload, he began to have more energy at night and would study Chinese or read his Bible. He'd also gaze at the photograph of his mother standing outside the factory in Guangzhou, as if focusing on it hard enough and long enough might somehow make her materialize or cause his belief in her to become manifest. He memorized every aspect of her profile and every line of her body and every characteristic of her features.

On the morning that marked one year since his arrival, Ethan went to speak to Zhou during breakfast. Ten minutes later, two of Zhou's men carried Ethan back into the room and dropped him onto his bedroll like he was a sack of trash. Ethan's nose was swollen and bleeding, and he cradled his right arm tightly to his chest.

"What happened?" asked Job.

"They said I owe them another six months," said Ethan.

"Why?"

"'Cause I'm too slow. And if I complain again, they said it'll be a year."

Before Job could say anything, another one of Zhou's men entered the room.

"*Kuài kuài*," he said.

The workers all quickly got up and followed Zhou's men to the assembly line. Job hesitated for a moment, looking at his wounded compatriot. Then he hurried off after the others.

He watched and he waited. A few weeks later, another man who'd been there for a year was told he owed another three months because his work was inferior. No one seemed to work well enough or fast enough to get released when they fulfilled their prearranged indenture, and anyone who tried to argue against it got their ribs or nose or jaw broken. Others agreed to commit more time in order to buy extra food or medicine or supplies or have money sent back to their families. Since he'd arrived, Job hadn't seen a single person leave, other than an older woman who'd died in her sleep. One morning, he noticed the cutter who'd trained him was gone. At breakfast, he overheard a few of the others talking about it.

"I heard they killed him."

"No way. Killed himself is more like it."

"Kyrah saw Zhou's men dragging him off."

"Kyrah's full of it."

"Then where is he?"

"Escaped."

"Bullshit."

"I heard he picked the lock on a door and then got out a window."

"Even if he did, they'll find him through the chip."

"Not if he cuts it out."

"You can't cut them out."

"Sure you can. I know a guy who cut his."

Job began to study the patterns and habits of Zhou's men. Which ones came at which times. How many there were at any time and if they carried weapons, and if so, what weapons they carried. He made little entries in code on a folded piece of paper with a pencil nub he'd found. He also began to study the building. He took note of its layout and its windows and its exits. He volunteered to load and unload the trucks whenever they came in and patched together a rough idea of the building's perimeter and its surroundings through an assortment of stolen and obstructed glimpses. At night, he added what he'd accumulated to his notes, and he studied the words and phrases Ynez had given him and studied Chinese newspapers and magazines he'd found at the factory as well, or he did push-ups and sit-ups. One day, he took a six-inch-long piece of a jigsaw blade when one of the jigsaws broke and hid it in his pant leg, and when he got back to the room they slept in, he hid it in a crack near the base of the wall. Another time, he took a flathead screwdriver that one of Zhou's men left on a work table and hid it at the bottom of his bedroll.

When it had been exactly one year since he'd been brought to the factory, Job requested to speak to Zhou. The men told him that Zhou was busy, so Job asked again the next day and got the same response. He kept asking them for eight days and finally one of Zhou's men brought him to an office. The room was a cluttered mess, filled with paperwork and laptop computers and other devices Job didn't recognize. A news program aired on a flat-panel screen on one wall, and Job felt pride in being able to understand every second or third word. Zhou sat at a desk watching the program and slurping a bowl of noodles; he spoke to Job without taking his eyes off the screen.

"What do you want?"

"I've been here a year."

"No, you haven't."

"Yes, I have."

"You don't make enough."

"I make more than anyone else—"

Zhou interrupted him. "We'll talk again in a few months," he said.

"Come on—"

Before Job could finish, the man who'd brought him there pulled him out into the hallway, where he punched Job in the gut. Job doubled over, sucking for air, and the man punched him hard in the side of the head. Job saw a blaze of hot stars; the man was wearing some sort of knuckle covers, and it felt like he'd been hit in the head with a metal pipe.

"*Kuài kuài*," said the man.

He yanked Job to his feet. Then he shoved him stumbling back toward the basement.

Job spent another month planning and preparing. Then he waited until the Saturday night before their next day off, when he knew the majority of Zhou's men would be out. He lay awake until two in the morning and then rose and got the piece of jigsaw and the screwdriver and his bedroll and made his way to the bathroom at the end of the hall. Once there, he closed the door behind him and took out the piece of jigsaw and began cutting through the wire covering the window. Before he got halfway through, he heard footsteps in the hallway. He got down and hid behind the door, gripping the screwdriver in his hand. Then he relaxed when he realized it was only Ethan.

"Are you crazy?" said Ethan.

Job said nothing.

"They'll kill you."

"Better all at once than drawing it out."

Without waiting for a reply, Job resumed cutting through the wire and when he was finished, he removed it from the window. Then he wrapped a T-shirt around his fist.

"Wait," said Ethan.

He left the room. For a moment, Job worried he might be going to tell Zhou's men, but a few seconds later, Ethan returned with his shoes and bedroll. He nodded, and Job nodded back. Then Job broke the window with his fist and then knocked out the shards of remaining glass in the frame.

Job climbed out the window, and Ethan followed. They crept their way across the lot, but before they got to the fence, a light came on behind them and then a door opened. One of Zhou's men came outside, shouting.

"Go!" shouted Ethan.

They sprinted toward the fence. As soon as he reached it, Job threw his bedroll over the concertina wire, covering it. Then he climbed over it, jumped down to the ground on the other side, and started running again. Ethan started up the fence after him, but Zhou's man grabbed one of his legs.

"Hey!"

Job stopped running when he heard Ethan shout and looked back to see Zhou's man yank Ethan to the ground. He hesitated for a moment, then turned and ran back toward the fence and climbed back over his bedroll. He jumped down and landed on the back of Zhou's man, shoving him to the ground. The man struggled to his feet, but Ethan tackled him at the waist. Together, he and Job pummeled the man until he stopped fighting back, and then Ethan kicked the man in the stomach once more for good measure. Job pulled the man's wallet from his pocket and climbed back over the fence, and Ethan climbed over the fence after him. Then they ran off as fast as they could.

As they approached an intersection, Job and Ethan heard an approaching car somewhere behind them, and then saw the arcing beams of a pair of headlights cutting through the darkness. Job turned to Ethan, and he knew from the look in Ethan's eyes that Ethan was thinking the same thing he was—that they'd have better chances if they split up.

"Good luck," said Ethan.

"You, too," said Job.

They ran off in opposite directions as the headlights grew larger behind them. At the end of the next block, Job saw an alley to his right. He turned up the alley and ran to its end before climbing another chain link fence and continuing on.

Then he kept running until his lungs ached and he was sure no one was still following him.

Job found an abandoned building and entered it through a boarded-up window. Inside the building, there was garbage everywhere and it smelled like an open sewer. It seemed unlikely that anyone would come looking for him there.

On the building's second floor, Job found a small and cluttered supply closet. The room had a grimy sink and mirror, and it stank of turpentine. He moved some boxes and buckets full of brackish water from the closet and then cleared out a space to sleep on the floor. Then he went inside and closed and locked the door behind him and then propped a board underneath the door handle in case anyone showed up with a key.

He took off his shirt and looked over his shoulder at his reflection in the mirror. Then he felt around for the chip in the center of his back, soon finding the lentil-sized bump between his shoulder blades. He used the jigsaw blade to make a small cut above the bump, then bit down on his T-shirt to prevent himself from shouting and used his fingernail to dig out the chip. The more he tried to dig it out, though, the deeper he seemed to push it in, but after a few tries, he finally managed to get it out.

Job looked at the bloody chip in his palm. It was silver and black and no bigger than one of the deer ticks he used to find crawling on him back home. He dropped it into the drain and then ran water over it. Then he rinsed his hands and dried them on his pants, put his shirt back on, and lay down and tried to sleep, but he could not, worrying that he'd made a mistake in leaving the factory. He tried to think of other things; at first he thought of his mother. Then Ynez came to mind, and he wondered where she'd ended up and if her experience had been like his had been, or worse.

He finally fell asleep just as the light from the rising sun was beginning to seep in through a crack underneath the door. He dreamed, and in his dreams, he was falling down a dark and endless well. At times, there were others falling along with him; at one point, Ethan was there flailing past him through the darkness, and at another point, Vargas was there and was sinking motionlessly like a stone. Then he saw Maddison, the woman from Salem with the strawberry hair. She opened her mouth to speak, but instead of words, a forked tongue spat out and reached out for him like a hand. When he finally woke that afternoon, it was to the sound of his own screaming.

He gathered his things and left the closet. Outside, the sun was beginning to set. While waiting for it to get dark, he went through the wallet of the man who'd chased them. He found some credit cards and what looked like a driver's license. The man's name appeared to be either Wan Xiaobin or Dante Xiaobin or Dante Xiao, or perhaps they were all right, or maybe they were all aliases. It didn't matter. There were also a number of colorful bills. Some of them had images of temples and mountains and rivers on back, and all of them had portraits of the same portly Chinese official on front.

He kept the money and put most of it into his pocket. Then he folded up and placed three of the notes under the sole of one his shoes. He put the credit cards and the driver's license back into the wallet and hid it in a box of trash. As soon as the sky darkened to the color of a bruise, he left the building.

Then he ventured out into the city.

Job found a bus stop at the end of the block and studied a map of the city's routes. It was complicated and confusing, and it looked like the nervous system of some strange alien creature. After a while, he figured out which direction the center of the city was, and he set out walking. At first, he avoided others and scuttled along the walls like a cockroach, but his confidence grew with every person who walked by without giving him a passing glance.

The buildings around him grew higher and higher the closer he got to downtown Dongguan. Everything seemed affluent and expansive and of a new age, and unlike anything he'd seen in the Americas. Colorful and futuristic vehicles cruised the streets, and the sidewalks grew thick with people. They weren't just from China, either; there were Koreans and Japanese and Malaysians and Filipinos, Australians and Pakistanis, pale northern Europeans and dark-skinned Africans, and manifold combinations of these and many more. They wore tailored suits and flowing robes and short dresses. Some talked on handheld devices or devices embedded in their ears; others studied tiny screens on watches, cell phones, or the insides of their glasses. All around them, enormous digital pitchmen moved across giant electronic billboards, promoting fast food and e-cigarettes and luxury automobiles in a multitude of languages. It was like something from a dream.

Job felt light and unfettered walking the city's wide-open streets after having been inside for most of a year. He took in the sights and sounds and smells all around him, the honking and talking and clanging music of industry, and the car exhaust and perfume and sizzling street food and sweat. He got distracted by a woman walking an enormous dog, and he walked headlong into a man pulling a large suitcase on wheels. The man nearly knocked him over and continued past without a glance. The city was enormous and sprawling and alive and new, and it made cities like Salem and Oakland seem like places from some quaint and outdated past.

He approached another bus stop and looked again at a map of the city. The main train station was only a few blocks away. He saw a surveillance camera pointing at him from a nearby light pole and instinctively moved out of its path, but then he saw another nearby, and then a few more small mounted devices that looked like cameras with panoramic, 360-degree capabilities, and he hurried on his way, realizing that it was pointless to try to avoid them.

On his way to the train station, he passed a produce market selling heaps of fresh grapes and cherries and watermelons and peaches, spiky durian and lychees and wax apples and dragon fruit. There were fruits and

vegetables he'd never seen, manmade varieties and breeds
that seemed impossible, like carrot grasses and black
tomatoes and some sort of berry tuber that grew in
bunches. He stared wide-eyed at noodle stalls and shops
that sold great golden moon cakes and mantou and jellies
set with agar, and he couldn't help but gape when a
gleaming orange sports car hovered past him as if riding
on air, its electric engine barely more audible than a
whisper.

He soon reached the train station and went inside.
Then he approached the ticketing windows and got in
line. He glanced around as he waited and noticed more
surveillance cameras and some policemen on patrol. They
wore shiny helmets and polished boots, and they carried
some sort of futuristic-looking sidearms or Tasers in
leather holsters. He also saw a few other Westerners there,
hustling about with mops and brooms or crates of fresh
flowers, and there were more stalls selling snacks and
magazines and cigarettes. One wall of the station was
covered with flyers advertising jobs and rooms for rent
and missing persons; another wall had listings that offered
Chinese lessons, promoted STD clinics, or offered to buy
organs.

After the customer in front of him finished his
business, Job approached the window, and a young female
clerk looked up at him. Her eyes were a startling shade of
pink.

"*Ni yao shen me?*" she asked.

He looked to his list of phrases and answered as best as he could, but the young woman didn't understand him. He repeated himself and pointed to Guangzhou on a map. She pressed something on the side of her neck and responded in English, and she began to speak with a British accent.

"What class?" she said.

"Whatever's cheapest," he said.

She printed a ticket for him and he paid her with some of his money. Then she pointed to the other side of the station.

"Track sixteen," she said, smiling and revealing a set of impossibly white teeth.

Job took his ticket and his change and walked over toward the other side of the station, where he checked a clock by a stairwell that led to a platform. His train wasn't due to leave for another fifteen minutes. He glanced around and noticed a man eating some sort of fried dumplings. His stomach grumbled; it had been nearly a day since he'd eaten. The smell was intoxicating; it reminded him of the wild boar piglets he and Eli had once found by the coast. They'd roasted them on spits and ate them tip to tail, picked the skeletons clean, and even made a stew with the ears and tails and feet. He went over to the food stall and bought some dumplings, quickly popping one into his mouth. It tasted like a cloud made of meat, greasy and rich yet still somehow light and better than anything he'd ever eaten. Then he saw someone nearby eating what looked like pudding with some sort of dark syrup. He went over to the stall where it was being sold and bought some of that as well. It tasted even better than the dumpling. He counted his remaining money and bought a second bowl of the pudding, and he soon began to feel sated for the first time in years.

Once he finished eating, Job made his way up to the platform and waited for the train. After a few minutes, it pulled into the station. Passengers disembarked and began to stream toward the exits, and as soon as they cleared off, he got on board. The train was spacious and clean and new and unlike the broken-down wrecks he'd been on back in America.

He found an empty seat near a window by the front of a car. There was a glossy magazine in the seatback in front of him, and he took it out and leafed through it. He couldn't understand many of the words, but the pictures were fascinating. Wealthy people in fancy clothes stood smiling before shiny cars outside palatial homes; others played games on horseback or rode down powdery, snow-covered mountains upon gleaming new skis. They reminded him of the advertisement he'd carried around in his grandfather's wallet since he'd been a boy, and he was glad to see that maybe that sort of life wasn't as fantastic as he'd once thought it to be.

A few minutes later, a man approached him and said something to him in Chinese. Job didn't understand, so the man repeated himself in accent-free English.

"That's my seat," he said.

"I'm sorry?"

"You're in my seat."

The man showed his ticket to Job, and then looked at Job's ticket before pointing toward the exit.

"You're in the next car," he said.

Job got his things and made his way down the aisle, where he passed through a sliding door. The seats were smaller in the next car, but they were still larger than any he'd seen on an American train. He found the seat corresponding to the number on his ticket and sat down, and a few minutes later, the electric train began to pull away from the station, floating as silently as a cloud.

He glanced out the window and watched as Dongguan receded into the distance.

Job arrived in Guangzhou just before midnight. The city was even larger than Dongguan; thickets of skyscrapers towered toward the sky, and elevated highways and train tracks crisscrossed the landscape in a dizzying matrix. In the distance, long strings of jet planes lined up to land at an airport, and scores of drones hovered above the city's thoroughfares, descending and ascending to deliver and collect packages.

He found a map of the city inside the train station's main terminal and looked for the Xi Xian factory, but he couldn't find it. He asked a few passersby in his clumsy

Chinese if they'd heard of it; none had, but one man pointed to an information desk on the other side of the terminal. Job approached the desk and asked for help, and the woman there gave him a map of Guangzhou and circled where the Xi Xian factory stood. She also told him which trains and bus lines he could take to get to that part of town.

Job left the station. The sidewalks and streets around the train station were a hive of activity despite the late hour, and he navigated his way through the hordes of people. Most were well-dressed Chinese and appeared to be out socializing or were just getting off work. There were also scores of foreign cab drivers and street cleaners and food vendors and deliverymen, mostly Africans and Caucasians, some of whose accents he recognized as Russian while others sounded Eastern European and American. Some heavily made-up and scantily dressed women whom Job assumed to be prostitutes lurked in alleyways or near parked cars, and like there were in Dongguan, there were surveillance cameras everywhere, which made Job believe the prostitutes were at least ignored if not outright allowed. He relaxed a bit more, though he remained watchful and on guard.

He made his way to a bus stop and waited for the next one to arrive. When it pulled up a few minutes later, he got on board and paid the fare. The bus soon pulled away from the stop, and he stared out the window as the city scrolled by. The sidewalks grew more and more sparse and the buildings grew smaller and smaller the farther away he got from the city center.

One by one, the passengers got off and dispersed into the night. When the driver finally pulled up to the station at the entrance to the Guangzhou Nansha Export Processing Zone, Job was the last one on board. He got off the bus and walked toward the Xi Xian factory. The streets around him were empty; at one point, a delivery truck rattled by as it made its rounds. He passed a man walking his dog and then he passed some Caucasian immigrants in sandals and rags who were rummaging through a trash can, but other than that, there was no one in sight.

He arrived at the gates of the Xi Xian compound just before dawn. He recognized it from the photograph he had, though it looked newer and larger in person and took up an entire city block. There were more than a dozen huge buildings inside the compound, and it was surrounded by a high wall crowned with black anti-scale fencing. He made his way to the main gate, where two armed guards sat in a sentry building, drinking tea and watching a wall of video monitors. One of them stood as Job approached.

Job took out the photo of his mother and asked in halting and broken Chinese if the guard knew her. The guard shot him a puzzled look, and Job asked again. The guard shrugged, so Job turned to the other guard and asked him, but the other guard shook his head. Job switched over to English.

"Is there anyone here who might know?" he asked.

Neither seemed to understand. Job tried one last time, and one of the guards pointed to his watch.

"*Qi dian zhong*," he said.

Then he held up seven fingers and repeated what he'd said, pointing again to his watch. Job went over and sat against the wall near one of the entrances and waited. At six forty-five, a number of managers began showing up at the factory gates; all but one of them were Chinese. Just before seven o'clock, one of the guards waved to Job from the sentry building.

Then he pointed to a balding man in a short-sleeved shirt and tie approaching the gate.

Job followed the man into a cramped office at the end of a hallway where a nameplate next to the door read "Ye Jitang." Reams of paperwork covered the man's desk; a container of murky tea stood next to a computer, and the room stank like stale cigarette smoke and milk that had gone bad.

"You speak Chinese?" asked Ye.

"A little," said Job.

"You're looking for work?"

Job shook his head.

"I'm looking for my mother," he said, taking out the photograph and showing it to Ye. "Her name's Merab Hammon."

"Sorry," said Ye.

"Please," said Job. "I know she was here."

"This isn't social services—"

Job interrupted him.

"I can pay you."

He pulled a fistful of bills from his pocket.

"I have almost five hundred here," he said.

Ye hesitated.

"Please," said Job.

"What's her name again?"

"Merab Hammon. She was here nine or ten years ago."

After a moment, Ye got up and closed the door. Then he picked up a phone on his desk and dialed a number. A moment later, someone answered at the other end, and Ye had a brief conversation with the other person in Cantonese. Job couldn't understand a word of what was said, and Ye laughed and shook his head before hanging up the phone.

"Well?" said Job.

"First the money," said Ye.

Job paid him, and Ye counted it before putting it away.

"Now take off your pants," he said.

"I beg your pardon?"

"You heard me."

Job hesitated.

"You're here illegally, aren't you?" said Ye.

"No."

"Then you won't mind if I call immigration?"

Job said nothing.

"It would be a shame if you were lying," said Ye. "You would be put on a ship and sent back to wherever you came from. Or worse."

Job hesitated again.

"Fine," said the man. "Have it your way." Ye picked up the phone again, but Job spoke before he could dial.

"Wait," he said.

"You want to know where your mother went?" said Ye. "Then take off your pants."

Job turned and looked out a window. In the far distance, an airplane began its long and slow descent toward the airport.

Job left the Xi Xian compound in the early afternoon. Outside, the sun lurked off to the west behind the overcast sky. He walked back in the direction of the bus stop, and when he got there, he sat down. It hurt, though, so he stood again and took off his shoe while standing. He noticed the sole was already coming apart, somehow even cheaper than the ones he'd been putting together in Dongguan.

He removed the money he'd hidden underneath his sole. Before long, a bus pulled up. Job put his worn shoe back on, boarded the bus, and paid the fare. Then he found an open space near the back door. He stood for the entire ride back to the main train station, repeating in his head as if a mantra the name of the Chongqing factory Ye had told him his mother had left for seven years before. After the bus arrived at the station, Job made his way to the ticketing windows and bought a one-way fare to Chongqing with most of his remaining money.

While waiting for the train to arrive, Job watched people buying dumplings and fried tofu and bowls of pudding at the food stalls. He counted the money he had left. Though his stomach was rumbling and he hadn't eaten all day, he thought it better to save what little he had.

After a few minutes, Job watched as a man tossed a half-eaten stick of meat into a trash bin. He made his way over to the trash can and fished out the food. Then he ate the cold tripe as quickly as he could. It tasted sour and had the consistency of rubber, but he was glad to have it.

As he forced down the food, Job watched two Chinese policemen rough up an old Caucasian beggar nearby. One of the policemen noticed Job, and Job turned and walked off before ducking into a restroom. He stood inside a bathroom stall until his train was scheduled to leave. He closed his eyes and whispered the Lord's Prayer to try to calm his nerves, but it didn't help, so he gave up. He then counted under his breath, as coldly and emotionlessly as a metronome. Once he assumed enough time had passed, he left the stall and made his way up to the platform.

A moment later, the train pulled up, and after the passengers disembarked, he stepped on board.

Pretty much everything that has ever lived on this earth has been on the move. Some things don't go all that far; there's a certain kind of red crab that only goes from one side of some small island to the other just to lay its eggs. I read that in a book I found in a box on a street corner. Other things go much farther. When I was little, Eli and I used to go to Depoe Bay every winter to watch the gray whales go past on their way down to Mexico. Until they stopped going past, that is. But when they were still around, they used to travel south every year, something like fourteen thousand miles round trip. They would swim all night and day for months at a time.

Then there are things that don't even finish the journeys they begin, like monarch butterflies. I read about them in another book. They reproduce along the way, and only the offspring of their offspring make it to wherever it is they're headed. They spend their entire lives on the way to somewhere else, never having a place to call home. Human beings don't seem to be all that different. I heard someone say the first Americans came over from Europe, and by the first Americans, I guess they meant the first white ones. There were already people here from other places, like the Inuit. They came from the Yukon and Alaska. The Nuxálk came from South America, and the Na-Dené were supposed to have come all the way from Siberia or something, thousands of years ago. A bunch came up from Mexico, too, but they're all pretty much long gone now, just like the gray whales. Died off or killed off or mixed in, or maybe just moved on again. I guess that's just the way it goes.

They say we all originally came from Africa, but I don't know about that. In Grandpa's Bible, it says that God created us on the sixth day in his own image out of nothing. I don't know about that, either. But what I do know is that we all probably came from somewhere else, and we'll all probably end up somewhere else, too.

We're more like dandelion seeds or something than things with roots.

IV

A jumble of skyscrapers began to appear in the distance, emerging from the wreck of a quartet of mountain ranges. As the train continued onward, the city swelled until it filled the horizon. Two murky rivers coursed their way through the endless panorama, converging at the shambling and gargantuan heart of it all. A logjam of tankers, cruisers, and steamboats navigated up- and downriver from the city's central port, carrying China's vast input and output in their massive holds.

The train arrived at the Chongqing Railway Station just as the sun was beginning to set behind a thick wall of fog. Job got off and merged with the bustling current of people surging toward the exits; he was pushed and shoved and jabbed and prodded, and he fought to keep up until he was finally disgorged from an exit tunnel and spat out into the city.

Once outside, he took in his surroundings. A riot of merchants, vendors, and food carts clustered around the station exits, hawking their wares. Herds of well-dressed office workers hustled up and down sidewalks on their ways out to dinner or home or to gyms or other after-hours destinations. Big, smoke-belching buses, gleaming town cars, and scores of taxis and motorcycles choked the busy avenues and boulevards, and drones rose and fell and rose again like horses on an amusement park carousel. The world was a cacophonous riot of car horns and industry and chatter, and a dizzying bouquet of diesel fumes and grease and sweat.

On the way from Guangzhou, Job had met another North American boy in the dining car. His name was Ren, and he was from a poor fishing village in former British Columbia. He wore dirty pajamas and a T-shirt that was too big for him, and his sneakers had yawning holes in the toes and soles. His left ear was mostly missing, and he talked with a lisp; though he appeared slow, his eyes were always darting around, as if he was constantly weighing and measuring things. He was going to Chongqing for work as his cousins had before him; Job asked him if he knew of the Yongtong radio factory, which Ye had told him that his mother had gone to. Ren didn't know of it, but he did have a large map of the city that one of his cousins had sent him. He helped Job locate the factory and determine what buses and subways to take in order to get to it, and they spent the night playing War and Go Fish and other simple card games with a dog-eared deck someone had left in a seatback. When they arrived in Chongqing the following day, they halfheartedly pledged to meet up again, though both knew they never would, as neither had any form of address, be it temporary or forwarding or even electronic.

Job made his way to the bus station and found the line to the New North Zone, where the Yongtong radio factory was. After a few minutes, a bus pulled up, and he got on board. It drove through hilly areas full of shopping malls, residential sky-rises, and lush green parks where locals did tai chi and practiced ballroom dancing. They passed through middle-class neighborhoods packed with schools, supermarkets, and homes for the elderly. They went through areas full of rickety slums and old tenements teeming with immigrants. The farther they got from the heart of the city, the more Chinese people got off the bus until the only passengers who remained were foreigners, destitutes, and the mentally ill.

Before long, a number of factories began to crop up along the wide avenues, towering and fenced-in structures of concrete and steel and glass. There were biopharmaceuticals factories and automobile plants, chemical refineries and garment makers. There were vast server warehouses and wind farms and solar panel plants;

it all seemed so wild and futuristic to Job, like it was some video game or a dream.

The bus pulled to a stop near the center of the industrial park, and the majority of the passengers filed off. Job got out and looked for the Yongtong radio factory. He found it at the end of a street near a plant that processed raw materials. There were lights on inside the factories, and people were still working even though it was approaching midnight; their shadows moved back and forth behind the windows like flies trapped in a jar, and the air outside smelled like sulfur and turpentine.

Job approached the main gate of the factory. A guard stood outside a sentry building, smoking an e-cigarette, while another sat inside the sentry building watching a bank of closed-circuit television monitors. Job approached the guard outside and took out the photo of his mother. He asked the guard in clumsy Chinese if he knew her, but the guard said nothing. Job switched over to English.

"Is there anyone who might know?" he said.

Again, the guard said nothing. Job pointed at the guard in the sentry building.

"*Qing wen?*"

The guard shrugged. Job approached the sentry house and asked the other guard in Chinese first and then in English. The guard spoke a little English but didn't recognize Job's mother from the photograph. He pointed toward a large message board near another one of the factory gates.

Job left the sentry building and approached the message board. Scores of flyers and listings were tacked to it. Some advertised Chinese lessons or job openings; others promoted employment agencies or health clinics. Most were missing persons flyers or notices posted by family members who'd been separated and were looking for one another. One had a photo of a family of four on it that was taken somewhere in the American Southwest; there were cacti and desert scrub outside a crumbling factory in the background. It read, "T.K. ELLS. LOOKING FOR VAN AND BREE. I HAVE A PHONE NOW. 139 1735 5135." Another had a picture of a boy who did not look much older than Job. It read, "DORRIT BLACK. LEFT HOME FOUR YEARS AGO. LAST SEEN AT XINSHANG METAL PROCESSING. PLEASE CALL OR E-MAIL."

There were hundreds more just like it, and he looked through them all, but none of them looked anything like his mother.

He spent the night behind a dumpster in a park. Afraid of being robbed or molested, he awkwardly slept against a cinder-block wall. The next morning, he woke when he felt a rat crawling across his hand. Instinctively, the thought of catching it and eating it crossed his mind, but it darted off and disappeared down a drainage culvert before he had the opportunity to do so.

After he got up and urinated in some bushes, he made his way to a number of food carts encamped around one of the factory gates. He spent half his remaining money on some sort of dumplings and pickled vegetables. They tasted greasy and bitter, but it was the first food he'd had since Guangzhou, and he was grateful for it.

After he finished eating, he went back to the entrance gate at Yongtong and watched as the managers and supervisors and office employees arrived. Like they were at Xi Xian, nearly all of them were Chinese. Another group of people were beginning to arrive, and they gathered in a loose queue and waited at one of the gates. They were Caucasian and Latino and African; most of them were young, and most of them seemed to be alone. They were skinny and dirty and shabbily dressed, and Job quickly realized they were there to get work.

He approached the queue of immigrants and got in line. Shortly before eight o'clock, a burly Chinese man accompanied by two guards emerged from the factory and approached them. The immigrants perked up and jockeyed for position and begged to be selected in clumsy Chinese or in their own native tongues. The man chose workers from the group by grabbing them by the shoulder and pushing them toward the factory; aside from a few teenage boys, he only selected young women.

Job pushed his way to the front of the pack and was one of the last ones chosen. He was brought with the others into building four of the number six factory at

Yongtong. The man who'd chosen them led them down a long hallway that smelled like mushrooms and cleaning fluid. They passed a number of dorm rooms where the immigrant workers were getting ready for the day; like the ones who were chosen with Job, most of them were young Caucasian women, and none of them were Chinese. They all looked tired and hungry and unclean, and the rooms weren't much better than the basement accommodations back at the sneaker factory in Dongguan. Strings of drying laundry crisscrossed the rooms, and the workers kept their meager and ratty possessions in backpacks or plastic garbage bags at the end of their bunks.

The man who'd selected them brought them into a canteen, where some of the workers were eating cold breakfasts of watery soup and congee and bananas and plain white rolls. He led them to a long steel table where they were all given tablet computers with some sort of electronic contract.

"Read these," he said. "Once you sign, you'll be given an ID card and assigned to a group."

Job looked at his screen. Everything was in Chinese; aside from the symbols for "man" and "corporation," he couldn't understand much. One of the other new workers signed with a large "X." Job looked over at a pair of older women who were eating breakfast; they had bags underneath their eyes, and they wore their stringy and graying hair tied back in loose knots. He wondered how old they were and if they were close to his mother's age.

Then he looked back at the tablet and signed the e-contract with his finger.

Job was assigned to a group working in quality control. His job was to check the solar panels as they moved past on the assembly line and to make sure the back contacts and antireflective coatings were properly affixed. It was monotonous, and the conveyor belt moved fast, but it was less dangerous than the job he'd held in Dongguan, and they only worked twelve hours a day instead of fourteen and got every Sunday off. Each shift, Job learned something else that had been on the contract he signed. Some things he learned from hearsay and some things he witnessed in action; the workers were required to stay for six months and the factory held the first three months' wages. Anyone who left before six months forfeited his or her back pay; anything a worker broke or any damaged product that a worker was responsible for was deducted from his or her pay. They were only allowed one five-minute restroom break every four hours; each additional break cost two hours' wages. Anyone late to work got docked a half day's wages, and any unauthorized day off forfeited one's wages for an entire week. All uniforms and towels and bedding came out of the workers' paychecks. If a worker got pregnant, it was grounds for immediate termination; theft and insubordination were also grounds for immediate termination. All of these penalties generally

169

whittled the workers' paychecks down to almost nothing and made it hard for them to leave. Despite all that, the conditions were far better than they'd been at the factory in Dongguan. There was hot water in the bathrooms. They didn't have to sleep on the floor. There was more food, and the quality of the food was better. There were fewer people to each room. They occasionally showed movies in the canteen at night, though they were in Chinese, and the workers were even allowed to leave the factory on their Sundays off.

Job kept to himself, and he did what he was told. He was given a bunk in a room with the other boys and a group of older women who were from South America and the Philippines. The women spoke Spanish and Portuguese and hung rosaries and prayer cards on the walls and on their bunks and played Canasta and Pusoy Dos and read dog-eared romance novels. The boys spent what little money they didn't send home on puffy down jackets and basketball sneakers and cigarettes and candy. One of them had a game console and the others piled onto his bunk after work and played fighting and first-person shooter games late into the night. Another started getting seizures in the morning and disappeared one Sunday while the others were gone; no one told them what had happened or were he'd gone, and no one bothered to ask.

On the first day he was there, Job began looking for his mother. He asked the women in his room and showed them her picture, but none recognized her. He asked everyone in quality control and everyone who worked on his line; none of them recognized her, either. He carried the photograph at all times and asked people in the canteen and in the hallway, and he asked the people he ran into in the bathroom and on the factory floor. At night, he went from room to room showing everyone the photograph, but no one knew who she was.

He began to realize that few people stayed at the factory for more than a year or two, so instead of asking if people recognized his mother, he started asking people who'd been at the factory the longest. Then he sought out those people and asked if they remembered his mother. He found someone who'd been there for four years, but she took one look at his photograph and shook her head. Then he heard about someone who'd been there for five years in one of the other buildings. On a Sunday evening, he sought the man out, but the man also didn't recognize his mother. He kept asking around and soon discovered there was someone who'd been there for almost eight years. When he found the old woman, he showed her the photograph of his mother. The woman stared at the photograph for a long time before finally speaking.

"Yes," said the woman. "I remember her."

Job felt his heart swell toward his throat.

"You know what happened to her?" he asked.

"There was a fight," said the woman. "Over pay, of course. She got docked for something that happened on her line, but she said it wasn't her fault, and when her manager refused to listen, she hit him with a wrench. Then security took her away."

"When was that?" asked Job.

"Six years ago, I think. Maybe seven."

"You know where she went?"

The woman shook her head.

"You know anyone who might know?"

"The only others who were working here then were Meracita and Janpen. You can try them."

Job sought out the other two women. Merecita did not remember the incident and did not remember his mother at all, but Janpen did; for a brief time, they'd even been in the same dorm room. But she didn't know what had happened to Merab after she left, as was generally the case with the factory workers; they moved in and out of each other's lives like buses at a busy station.

Job continued to work the line. He continued to look for his mother as well, but he found no one who'd had a longer tenure than Merecita or Janpen or the old woman. On the morning marking six months since his arrival, he went to see his manager. The man was in his thirties and wore thick glasses, and he smelled like chicken grease and ravaged the female employees with his eyes.

"I want to leave," said Job.

"Why?"

"Never mind why. Just give me my back pay."

"Stay through the season."

"No, thanks."

"I'll give you your back pay if you stay through the season."

Job argued for a while longer but realized it was futile—he wasn't getting his back pay, no one did—so he left the manager's office and returned to his dorm. A few days later on his Sunday off, he went to another section of the city called Little Tokyo, where he heard there were dozens of Japanese robotics factories. On a billboard near a park, he found scores of other missing persons flyers. One was scrawled on the inside lid of a cardboard box; "LOOKING FOR GAILY EVERT. PLS CALL 419 9765 4923," it read. Another had "HAVE YOU SEEN THIS PERSON?" written over a photograph of an acne-scarred teenage girl. There were more advertisements for Chinese lessons and courses in Java and C# and Falcon and other programming languages. There were also dozens of flyers announcing job openings and work opportunities.

Job took a few of the flyers and went looking for employment. He got hired at the third factory that he went to, a Japanese manufacturer that produced electronic components. He was given another small bunk in another cramped room full of more spinsters and boys. The person who led him to his bunk cleared away the scant belongings of its former occupant, and as he did so, Job imagined that the same thing was happening at that same moment to his own toothbrush and towel back at Yongtong.

The managers at the electronics factory were all
Chinese and Japanese, and the workers were mostly
African and Malaysian and South American. Instead of
quality control, Job worked in packaging. He earned more
than he'd earned at Yongtong, but the workers there were
docked more for being late and for unauthorized absences.
The uniforms, towels, and bedding were free, but the food
was miserable, and the factory floor smelled like machine
lubricant and acetone and gave him blinding headaches.

Before his first month there had ended, he'd already
begun looking for other work.

Job spent another six months hopping from one factory to
the next. Eventually, he realized that though the factories
had superficial differences, they were all more or less the
same. Some produced electronics while others made
clothes. Some had African and South American workers
while others had Caucasians. Some paid more but charged
for everything, while others paid less but charged little.
Some had fumes that made him sick, while others had
work that gave him blisters or burns or had mattresses full
of lice. None gave back pay and nowhere did he find
anyone who knew his mother.

He finally settled at another solar panel factory
because the pay was the best, though the hours were the
longest. During that time, he'd grown another two inches,
gained another ten pounds of muscle, and had to buy

more new clothes. He'd grown more hair under his armpits and on his legs and chin as well; he spent little and kept to himself, and he did what he was told. On Sundays off, he wandered the city showing the photo of his mother to any Caucasian strangers he ran into and asked if they knew her or had seen her, but none of them had.

The more time he spent wandering the city, the more he saw and learned. He watched the locals and studied their habits and picked up some more Chinese and even some of the local Sichuanese dialect. He watched the police and saw which immigrants they hassled and which they left alone, and why. He learned all of the bus routes and the subway routes and how to buy a pass for both. He learned which neighborhoods were immigrant friendly and which weren't, and he also began noticing how many Caucasians worked as dishwashers and deliverymen and taxi drivers and prostitutes.

One day while asking people if they'd seen his mother, Job spotted a boy named Cantey he knew from the Yongtong factory, riding a delivery service scooter. He was wearing an orange-and-black uniform, and he looked like he'd put on some weight since Job had last seen him. Cantey parked the scooter outside an apartment building and took out an insulated delivery bag from a container strapped to the back of the scooter. Then he carried the bag into the building.

Job watched and waited. After five minutes, Cantey came back out with the empty delivery bag, and Job approached him. Cantey immediately recognized him, and they caught up. Job asked Cantey how he'd become a courier; Cantey told him that the man who hired the couriers was a friend of a friend, and through that friend, he'd given the man a bribe of about a month's wages from his last job. The next day, he got called in and was given the job. Job said it seemed like a lot of money to pay for work, but when Cantey told him how much he was making, the payment didn't seem like that much to make at all.

"That's how they do it," said Cantey, flicking his spent cigarette butt to the street. "You gotta spend money to make money."

Job finished out his six months at the panel factory. Like he'd done at Yongtong, he went to see his manager on the day that marked it and told him he wanted to leave. The manager said his performance was too poor for him to receive his back pay; Job protested, but his manager refused to budge. Job finally gave up, but not before he'd managed to take his manager's gold wristwatch, which had been sitting atop his desk.

After collecting his things, Job left the factory. He got on a bus and then a subway and rode to the other side of the city, toward Koreatown and Americatown and

Zhongliangshan and Little Moscow. At one point, a pair of policemen stepped onto his subway car. He felt one of them staring at him, and he closed his eyes and waited for the worst, but two stops later, he opened his eyes and was relieved to see them gone.

The train pulled to a stop at the Immigrant City station and Job got off and made his way to the exit. Out on the street, merchants were selling Mexican and Malaysian street food off rickety card tables and food carts. Others sold drugs and stolen batteries and tablets, while prostitutes and massage parlor girls beckoned clients from shabby storefronts and club entrances.

Job soon found a number of pawn shops on a street running beneath an illuminated highway overpass. Their display windows were all barred, and they were filled with used electronics and jewelry and high-end medical devices. A homeless Caucasian beggar sat sleeping against the wall in between two of the larger shops; his dirty skin was scabbed over with a tapestry of reddish black carcinoma and his long hair and beard were nests of filth. It was hard to tell whether he was still living or not, and Job shuddered, seeing his brother for a moment in the man.

He entered one of the pawnshops. He chose it when he saw a Caucasian man standing behind the counter, rather than an African or an Asian. A muscular Rottweiler sleeping on a bed in one corner of the room lifted its head and sniffed at the air when Job entered before lying back

177

down. The proprietor looked up from a magazine full of semi-nude Japanese schoolgirls in erotic positions and addressed Job in Chinese.

"You speak English?" asked Job.

"Little bit," said the man, speaking with an accent that Job couldn't place.

Job took out the watch and set it on the countertop.

"How much will you give me for this?" he said.

The man picked up the watch and looked it over. Then he shouted something in what sounded like Russian toward someone in a back room. A moment later, another man entered from the back. He was taller than the proprietor but had similar features and looked like he could have been a brother or a cousin. They argued in their native language for a moment and then the proprietor turned back to Job.

"I give you one thousand," he said.

"No way."

"One thousand is good price."

"This watch is gold."

"So what?"

"So give me twenty-five hundred."

The man laughed and muttered something in his native tongue.

"Give me two thousand, then," said Job.

"I give you twelve fifty."

"You'll make five times that selling this."

"I am guessing that is more than you paid for it," said the man. "Or am I wrong?"

"Give me eighteen hundred."

"I give you thirteen."

"Make it sixteen."

"Thirteen fifty. Final offer."

Job hesitated for a moment and then nodded. He looked over at the sleeping Rottweiler as the man began to count bills off a thick roll. The dog's eyes darted back and forth beneath its eyelids, and its legs twitched as it chased something in its dreams.

Job went to a nearby park and found an empty bench. He put his jacket beneath his head and closed his eyes, but he couldn't fall asleep. After tossing and turning for hours, he finally dozed off, and in his dreams he was treading water in some dark and bottomless ocean, and then he was fighting what seemed like a giant octopus, and though he kept pushing it away, it kept coming back at him, and then he suddenly woke up and it was dawn, and two homeless Caucasian men were rifling through his pockets. He kicked and lashed out at them, and they drunkenly backed off. Then Job grabbed his things and hurried away.

It was still early, so he took the subway back toward a safer part of the city and found a crowded expanse of grass and benches near the foreign embassies. Local pensioners and the elderly were playing mah jong or practicing tai chi or qigong or bartering over fresh produce lying out upon pieces of cardboard. Nearby vendors sold jiaozi and pancakes and shizibing and other Sichuanese breakfast foods. He bought a few of the cheapest ones, and though the sticky fillings were far too sweet for him, he ate them anyway, not wanting to waste money. He washed the food down with half of a bottle of tea that someone had left lying by a trash can, then leafed through a section of discarded newspaper he'd found.

Once the sun was up, Job found a pay phone and called Cantey, but the call went straight to Cantey's voicemail. He went back to the park, and for a while, he watched a man fight with a wooden sword against an invisible foe and listened to the chattering of the pensioners' caged thrushes and mynah birds. He soon saw a businessman throw away half of a shizibing, and he went and fished it out from the trash and wrapped it in a napkin and put it away with the rest of his things. Then he went back to the bank of pay phones and called Cantey again, and this time Cantey answered, and Job asked him if he could help him get work.

Job met Cantey in the afternoon at the location of one of Cantey's deliveries. Cantey took Job's money and told him to meet him back at the same place at the same time the following day. Job spent the rest of the afternoon wandering Americatown and Little Manila and the French

Quarter and some of the other enclaves of foreigners. He asked the people he ran into if they recognized his mother from his photograph. After numerous failures, he met someone who said they did recognize her, but he realized the person was mistaken when he called her Zlata and said that she was Bosnian.

When night came, Job made his way back to the park near the foreign consulates and embassies. He ate the half of the cold shizibing he'd saved and then went from trash can to trash can collecting plastic bottles and aluminum cans. After he took them to a recycling center and turned them in for their refunds, he thought about buying a bowl of soup from one of the food stalls, but he decided instead to save the money and promised himself he'd buy breakfast the following morning. Then he went back to the park and found an empty bench to sleep on.

After a while, he started to doze off, but then the thought occurred to him that Cantey had swindled him. He tried to remember the boy from their time together at Yongtong; he couldn't remember him that well or whether or not he was trustworthy or if he'd stolen anything from the factory or anyone else. He began to wonder why Cantey was helping him and what might be in it for him, and the more he thought about, it the more stupid he felt. He imagined Eli berating him for falling for such a ruse, and he grew disgusted with himself.

He lay awake all night and was still awake when the first fingers of dawn began to spread across the sky. Before long, the food stalls started setting up for the day, but he decided against buying breakfast, fearing his situation was about to get worse and that he'd need the money later. He waited until he saw a man throw away part of a pancake and then went over to the trash can to retrieve it, but when he reached in, he ended up getting dog feces all over his hand. Dejected, he made his way to the restroom at the subway station and washed there. Then he took the subway back to the area of town where Cantey had told him to meet.

The time they'd arranged to meet came and went, and then a half hour passed, and then another half hour. Job went to a pay phone and called Cantey, but it went straight to his voicemail. At first, he felt enraged; getting robbed or used by strangers was one thing, but getting taken advantage of by a friend was far worse. Then he grew even more dejected. Before long, a bus approached in the distance, and the thought of stepping in front of it suddenly entered his mind. The notion took his breath away; he'd never contemplated suicide, but now he had, and it was so easy to consider, and almost even enticing.

He felt the urge to cry for the first time since leaving Ellendale. He seemed to be no closer to finding his mother, and the thought of going back to the factories was unbearable. Going home was out of the question, too, but even if it wasn't, there was nothing for him to go home to. He suddenly began to realize why so many immigrants ended up in jail or homeless, or became drug addicts or prostitutes, or just stayed in the voluntary prisons of the factories.

He stifled the urge to cry and considered his options. He could look for Cantey, he could look for more work, he could go back to Yongtong, or he could rob someone. None of these options appealed to him, though, so he closed his eyes. His mind raced with dark thoughts, so he began counting to himself to crowd them out.

After reaching a count of a hundred, he heard the blast of a bus horn. He opened his eyes to see a bus approaching, and then a car, and then a pair of mopeds and a truck full of melons. A moment later, an orange-and-black scooter appeared in the bustling traffic, splitting the lanes as it approached.

At first, the rider didn't look like Cantey, but as the moped neared, Job realized with great relief that it was him.

Cantey apologized for being late. There'd been a rush for deliveries and he'd ended up having to take a number of orders of steak tartare and hand-rolled sushi over to the new luxury sky-rises overlooking the Yangtze. He gave Job a business card with the address of a delivery service office in the Yuzhong District and told him to go there at four o'clock and to ask for Lee Jun Fan. If Lee Jun Fan liked him, the job was his. In his time as a courier, Cantey had seen some boys who'd paid get hired and some who'd paid not get the job, so it wasn't a sure thing, but it was a chance, and that was more than Job had anywhere else.

He took the subway downtown and got to the office an hour early. He waited outside until it was four o'clock and went in and was told to wait again. At five o'clock, the door to a back office finally opened, and out came an older man in a suit, followed by a sinewy, middle-aged man with an intricate dragon tattoo that started at his wrist, curved around his arm, and went up his neck, where it ended behind his right ear. The tattooed man was sucking on a vape pen, and he wore a tight black T-shirt and pants and had a thick cataract over one eye. He asked in Chinese if Job was Cantey's friend, and Job nodded. Then he turned and went back into his office, trailed by the sickly sweet exhalation from his vape pen.

Job quickly followed him inside. The office was no bigger than a storage closet, and it was filled with computers and bookshelves crammed with files and stacks of restaurant menus. More restaurant menus and paperwork covered a small desk, and there was so much smoke that it was hard to see from one side of the room to the other.

Li Jun Fan spoke with a thick Sichuanese accent and studied Job with his one good eye as if looking over the engine under the hood of a car. He asked Job if he knew how to operate a scooter, and Job nodded. He told Job the hours were ten in the morning until midnight with a break for lunch in the afternoon. A courier had forty-five minutes to make a delivery anywhere in the city at any time; if a courier was late, the order was free, and it came out of his pay. Three late orders in a month, and a courier was terminated. All couriers got a day rate plus tips; a good courier could make three or four times what a factory worker made, if not more. The best couriers got the best routes and the regular customers, which led to more deliveries and even more tips. Lee Jun Fan asked Job if he had any questions, and Job shook his head. Then Lee Jun Fan lowered his voice and told Job that the couriers who wanted to keep their positions gave him a quarter of their tips at the end of each month. Having started himself as a courier, Lee Jun Fan knew what couriers generally received for tips, so he knew when couriers were holding back. He asked if Job wanted the position, and when Job told him he did, he told Job to be there at ten o'clock the next day and waved him away with one hand before turning his attention to a computer screen.

Job bounded down the building's stairs, leaping them two and three and even four at a time. He felt light and electric and as if he was walking on air. As soon as he was outside, he made his way to a pay phone. Then he called Cantey, and after the third ring, Cantey picked up.

"How'd it go?" asked Cantey.

"Great," said Job, then added: "Can you teach me how to drive?"

At midnight after Cantey finished his shift, he met Job at the pedestrian mall in downtown Jiefangbei. They rode out to an empty parking lot near Datianwan Stadium, and Cantey showed Job how to operate a scooter. He demonstrated how to change gears, how to accelerate, and how to use a hand brake. At first, Job had some difficulty, but he soon got the hang of it, and by the time they left Datianwan, he could operate the scooter with ease.

They rode back to the Americatown slums where Cantey had been living since leaving the factory. The crowded and dirty streets there were filled with cramped stalls and graffiti-tagged storefronts and jerry-built wet markets selling dirt-covered produce, knockoff medications, and no-brand clothes. A fat man in a T-shirt fished gray frankfurters from a cloudy pot of boiling water and shoved them into buns before handing them off to his customers; another man cooked up some sort of greasy and Americanized fusion of fried rice, spaghetti, and Spam. People sat in small groups on plastic lawn chairs and stools outside tiny open apartments that looked dirtier than the streets themselves and watched tablet computers or mended clothes or picked through mounds of unshelled beans. Toddlers in dirty clothes and slit pants played in alleyways and on sidewalks. The area had the boisterous and transitory feeling of a refugee settlement or military encampment.

They parked the scooter by a rack jammed with mopeds and e-bicycles. Cantey locked it to the rack with a thick steel padlock and chain, and they made their way up an alley and into a maze of back lanes and narrow passageways. At the back exit of an apartment building, a man sold stolen electronics. A tattooed junkie nodded off behind a dumpster with a needle still stuck in his arm, and at the end of an alley, a prostitute gave head to an Asian man in a track suit.

They approached a run-down building catty-corner from a fast food restaurant selling fried chicken and egg rolls. Cantey typed in a code on a keypad and a door unlocked, and they entered a grimy foyer. The elevator was broken, so they made their way up a dark and fetid stairwell. A brothel run by Russians occupied the second floor of the building, and some sort of illegal abortion clinic took up much of the third.

They exited the stairwell when they reached the fifth floor, and Job followed Cantey toward a wooden door with a large and jagged "E" cut into it. Cantey opened the door, and Job followed him inside. In the main room of the apartment, two teenage boys slept on bare mattresses, and another boy lay in a sleeping bag on the floor.

"That's Jeris and Vonta," said Cantey, nodding to the boys on the mattresses. "The one on the floor's C. C."

The boys grunted as Cantey continued down a hallway toward two closed doors. Job followed. They passed a cramped kitchen on their right; dirty plastic dishes and cups filled a sink, and the small countertop was covered with cereal boxes, half-filled soda bottles, and plastic bags of white bread.

When they reached one of the doors, Cantey turned to Job.

"Me and Nazr sleep in here," he said. "You can share my bed until someone leaves."

Job nodded toward the other door.

"What's in there?" he asked.

"That's the bathroom."

"You have your own bathroom?"

Cantey nodded.

"Use it whenever you want," he said. "Just don't leave shit in the toilet."

As Cantey began shucking off his shoes, Job approached the bathroom and went inside. He turned on the light and closed the door behind him, then turned on the faucet. The water ran clear, and a moment later, it grew warm and then even became hot.

Job shook his head but couldn't help but smile.

The following morning, Job rode with Cantey to a market that sold knockoff goods. He bought a pair of black lace-up boots there and immediately threw his rotting shoes into a trash can. Then he put the new boots on and looked down at them, beaming. He'd never owned new boots before, least of all matching ones, and he felt like an entirely new person.

They left the market and rode to the delivery service office. When he got there, he was given the keys to a rust-eaten 50cc scooter, a cheap GPS device, and a used orange-and-black uniform two sizes too big for him that smelled like ketchup and sweat. After he put on the uniform, he went to the dispatch department and clocked in with the other couriers. Then he listened to them talk with each other about the previous day's deliveries and who got the best tips and what streets to avoid.

The first order of the day came through at ten fifteen. It was called in by a regular customer who tipped well, and it was given to one of the senior couriers. The next order came in a few minutes later and was for food from a teppanyaki restaurant over by J-Town. Because the order was small and because there was little chance of a tip, it was given to Job. Cantey approached him before he left.

"You have enough cutlery packs?" he asked.

Job nodded.

"How about the *fapiao*?"

Job nodded again.

"You'll want to avoid the expressway," said Cantey. "The surface streets are much better."

Job went outside and found his scooter. He slid the key into the ignition and turned it, but it wouldn't start. He tried again and again, but still nothing happened. He adjusted the choke and tried one more time, and the engine finally sputtered to life.

He climbed onto the scooter and rode off. The streets were a snarl of activity. Taxis sped honking through intersections and buses went barreling past, and scores of other couriers and riders choked the narrow garbage-filled shoulders. He arrived at the restaurant just before eleven o'clock. A woman stood at the reservation desk and had the order waiting for him; cursing in some dialect he didn't recognize, she pointed to her watch when he came in.

"Sorry," he said.

She berated him as he took the order. Then he went back outside, where he put the food in his insulated delivery bag strapped to the back of the scooter. He looked at the time on his GPS device; he'd already spent twenty minutes getting there, and he now only had twenty-five minutes to get the food to J-Town, which was almost halfway across the city.

Job got on the scooter and slid the key into the ignition. This time, the engine started on the second try. He pulled off into traffic, and a taxi blasted its horn as it approached. He swerved to avoid getting hit and jumped the curb and briefly went up onto the sidewalk before dropping back down onto the street again. His heart hammered in his chest, and he checked his cracked and dirty side-view mirrors before continuing.

He navigated through the sea of traffic on his way to J-Town, narrowly avoiding getting into a number of accidents and getting honked at and sworn at by a number of other drivers. An accident between a taxi and a moped at the intersection of two busy thoroughfares slowed him down, and he tried to make up the lost time by heading toward a parallel street, but he got sidetracked in a labyrinth of one-ways. By the time he saw the building where the order was to be delivered, it was approaching forty-five minutes since the order had been made.

He parked the scooter and locked it to a sign. Then he took the insulated delivery bag from the back of the scooter and hurried toward the building entrance. The lobby was cavernous and filled with cool clean air that smelled nothing like the air in the city; it smelled like nothing at all, actually, which was what made it seem so strange. A doorman stopped him from going to the elevator and rang up to the tenant to get permission to let him up. As he stood there waiting, Job glanced at the time. It was forty-six minutes since the order had been made, and he was now officially late.

After a moment, the doorman hung up the phone and allowed Job through. Job approached a bank of elevators and waited for one to come. When it finally arrived, he stepped in and took it to the seventeenth floor. It had floor-to-ceiling mirrors and was almost bigger than the room that he'd slept in at Cantey's apartment.

When the elevator arrived on the seventeenth floor, he got out and approached the door to the apartment and rang its buzzer. After a moment, a fat Chinese boy with spiky orange hair who seemed younger than him opened the door to reveal the large foyer of a massive floor-through apartment. A graphic image of an alien's head exploding by a shotgun blast filled a huge, flat-screen television that nearly took up an entire wall; another wall showed a view of the city that looked like the views on the postcards Job saw at the corner markets, and catchy Cantopop blasted on a stereo somewhere in the background.

"*Ni hao*," said Job.

The boy said nothing, only interested in his food and not the faceless *laowai* bringing it to him. Job took the items from the insulated bag one by one as he had been instructed and began to pass them to the boy, but the boy grew impatient and snatched them all at once. When Job handed the boy the bill, the boy paid him with a fistful of crumpled notes and slammed the door in his face.

Job counted the money as he made his way back to the elevator. The boy had given him exact change.

Job went outside and found a pay phone nearby and called the dispatch department. He was relieved when they gave him his next order without saying anything about his being late for the last one; the boy either hadn't noticed or hadn't cared. He spent the rest of the afternoon hustling back and forth from Yangjiaping to Qinjiagang to Jiulongpo to Tongguanyi, delivering short ribs and toro sashimi and duck liver pâté and all sorts of foods he'd never tried nor even heard of. The apartments he delivered to were huge and well furnished, and the bills of the orders were often more than he made in a week and sometimes even more than he made in a month.

At the end of the lunch shift, he went back to the delivery service office. The other couriers were already there having their own lunches; they ate steaming bowls of lamian at a cheap noodle stall next to the office, and they sat outside on stools and discussed the deliveries they made and the tips they got or didn't get and the traffic and the attractive new girl who was working for Lee Jun Fan. One of the couriers had been hassled that morning by the police and almost ended up being late for a delivery, and another courier had made a delivery where a man came to the door naked and high on something. After lunch, they all went back up to the dispatch department, and before long, the early dinner orders began coming in. Job got his first order and went out to Huxi and then on to Shiqiaopu and Gele Shan and Huayan. He delivered baby tiger prawns and filet mignon and deep-fried cuttlefish and imported champagne. The people he delivered to lived in sky-rise penthouses and walled mansions and renovated lane houses, and they had immigrant maids and butlers and doormen attending to their every need.

On his second-to-last delivery of the day, Job got an order to bring two pizzas to an apartment building in Shapingba. When he rang the buzzer to the door, a middle-aged Caucasian woman answered. He could tell she was American by her accent and by some of the things in the apartment. Two young Asian Caucasian children were sitting behind her on a large couch, watching an animated film about a mermaid on a large flat-screen TV.

Job gave the pizzas to the woman, and she paid him in cash. When he went to give her her change, she smiled as if somehow knowing or pitying or perhaps both and told him to keep it. He smiled and left the building. Once outside, he called the dispatch department for his last order and picked it up and delivered it to the customer. He felt like he was flying on his way back to the delivery office. When he got there, he checked his orders with the woman in the dispatch department. Then he went with the other couriers to a food stall in Americatown and ate heaping plates of noodles and chili and rice and drank watery beer and listened to their stories until the sun finally came up.

Job got paid at the end of the week. They deducted some for his uniform and some for a delivery that was a few minutes late. Of the remainder, he gave Lee Jun Fan his cut and some to Cantey and the others for rent. Then he spent a bit on some breakfast cereal and toothpaste and hid the rest under the sole of his boot.

Jeris left the apartment three weeks after Job had moved in; he'd gotten an offer from a friend for a better-paying job in Chengdu. The week after that, another new boy moved in with them; his name was Shem and he was from Northern California and he was new to China and had just gotten hired at the restaurant where Vonta bussed tables. He had crooked yellow teeth, mismatched shoes, and a cagey, wild look in his clear blue eyes, and when Job looked at him he couldn't help but think that he was looking at his own warped and recent past as if in the reflection of some sort of time-traveling funhouse mirror.

Three weeks after Shem moved in with them, Nazr disappeared. He didn't come home from work one night and he didn't come home the following night or the night after that, and he didn't call any of them to tell them what had happened, if anything had happened, or where he was going or if he was going anywhere. After a week, they all assumed he'd either gotten a better job or gone home or had been caught by immigration or worse, and they divvied up his things. C. C. took over the unoccupied mattress and Shem moved from his place on the floor to the mattress C. C. had been sharing with Vonta. There was a natural and unspoken law among them, as if a law of survival that animals obeyed in the wild.

Job learned about disposable cell phones with pay-as-you-go plans from one of the other couriers. He bought the cheapest he could find with the cheapest plan available and got his own number. Within minutes, he committed it to memory. The first chance he could get, he made photocopies of the picture of his mother outside the Xi Xian factory and circled her and wrote his number on it along with the words "LOOKING FOR MERAB HAMMON—PLS CALL." Then he began posting them up on the message boards scattered all over the city.

A week went by. Then another week, and then another. He finally got a call after four weeks had passed, but when he answered the phone, he heard a recorded message at the other end, from a company looking for salesmen. Not wanting to waste any of his precious minutes, he hung up the phone before the recording finished playing. Then he went back to the photocopier and made more copies of his mother's picture.

He rode every day and every night from one end of the city to the other, delivering meals to the wealthy. He became adept at driving in the heavy fogs that frequently blanketed Chongqing as well as the drenching rains that regularly washed it clean. He went from the clustered skyscrapers in hilly downtown Jiefangbei to the old stilted houses in Chongqing City and from the fancy apartments overlooking the southern bank of the Yangtze to the sprawling suburbs in the north that clustered around the airport. He learned the vast network of ring roads and highways and bridges, and he learned how to avoid the steep and congested areas and where the shortcuts were. The more he rode, the quicker he got at navigating the city and the more deliveries he was able to make and the more money he earned. The more he rode, the more places he was also able to post his mother's picture, and when the first pictures he put up began fading or getting torn down or covered over, he made new copies and posted them in their place.

After a few months, he got a phone call from a man who said in Chinese that he'd seen his mother. When Job asked for details, the man asked Job what was in it for him. He told the man he didn't have much money, and the man snorted and hung up. Job tried to call him back, but it had been an unlisted number. A month later, he got another call from a woman who said she knew his mother. She spoke English with an American accent and sounded like a heavy smoker, and when he asked her where his mother was, she said she was sorry to have to be the one to break it to him but that the woman in the photograph was dead. Job asked for more information, but the woman didn't have any, and she hung up. When Job tried to call her back, she didn't answer, and there was no voicemail for him to leave a message.

On his rare days off, Job began to visit morgues. He asked the people who worked there if they'd seen any unclaimed bodies that looked like his mother or if they had anyone named Merab Hammon in their systems. None did. He also began visiting cemeteries in poor sections of town that had unmarked plots set aside for immigrants and the poor, and he asked the people there if they'd seen any dead women who'd looked like his mother or if they'd buried anyone named Merab Hammon, but none had. He soon discovered that most of the immigrants who died and whose bodies were not immediately claimed were promptly cremated, and where their ashes ended up was a mystery. They lived invisible lives, and they died invisible deaths much in the same fashion that they'd lived.

He took as many extra shifts as he could and started to work holidays and Sundays as well. He never missed his payments to Lee Jun Fan and even rounded up instead of down, unlike the other couriers. After six months, he started receiving some of the better customers and some of the better routes, and after nine months, Lee Jun Fan began paying him to train new couriers. Job spent every moment he could around Lee Jun Fan, listening to his stories and asking him questions and for advice. The more liberal he got with his payments to Lee Jun Fan, the more generous Lee Jun Fan was with his time and experience. Job even learned a bit about Chinese history, about how communism had stripped everything away to start anew, and that the first thing they'd opened back up in the great void were the markets, which was why money meant everything—it was China's religion, and it was the basis of everything in its culture. If Job wanted to understand and succeed in China, Lee Jun Fan said, then he needed to understand that before all else.

After a year, Job found a small room for rent in a one-bedroom apartment in Americatown that had been converted into a three-bedroom apartment by a couple of other couriers. The room was only half as big as the room he was sharing with Cantey and Jimmy, and it was no bigger than a closet, but it would be all his and it wasn't much more than he was already paying. He moved in just before his seventeenth birthday; it was unfurnished, and he didn't have enough money for a mattress or even a sleeping bag, but he had a room of his own for the first time in his life. On his seventeenth birthday, he bought a sleeping bag and some pants. He also bought a box of butter cookies and ate them all in one sitting. With the rest of his money, he made more copies of the photo of his mother, then went out the following morning before work and resumed posting them all over the city.

Two more seasons came and went without any more phone calls about his mother, other than an occasional solicitor, pervert, or wrong number. The suffocating summer humidity returned to Chongqing and then left again. One Sunday morning before going to work, Job rode out to post fliers by the new developments and factories of the Yubei District. After posting one on a message board near the gate of an aluminum plant, he saw a young woman lying facedown in an alley. The woman's pants were torn and stained, and her long black hair was a tangled mess, and he normally would've walked right past her, but there was something about her that seemed familiar, something nagging but vague. Then he saw the purple birthmark on the right side of the young woman's neck, and he immediately realized it was Ynez, as impossible as it seemed. All the feelings he'd had for her flooded back into him, and his heart swelled into his throat.

Job knelt down and turned Ynez onto her back. He couldn't believe how light she was; her body felt like a bag of sticks. At some point since he'd seen her, her face and arms had been badly slashed and were now crisscrossed with a lattice of knotty white scars. Raw red needle marks ran up and down the lengths of her skinny arms, her cracked lips were blue, and dried vomit and blood caked the front of her shirt. He put his ear next to her chest and listened for a heartbeat, but he heard nothing. She was so thin that he could feel her ribs against his ear, and her skin was as clammy as lunch meat.

"Ynez?" he said.

She didn't reply. He gently slapped her.

"Wake up," he said.

Again, she didn't reply, so he slapped her harder.

"Come on," he said. "Wake up."

He began to shake her, but when she still didn't respond, her shook her even harder.

"Ynez!" he shouted.

He shook her as hard as he could until she finally seized up and pitched forward. Then she opened her mouth and promptly vomited into his lap. She continued to throw up until she had nothing left to give, and then she began dry heaving, her thin body twisting like a towel being wrung dry. She looked up at his face and stared through him with glazed and bloodshot eyes. He couldn't tell if she recognized him or not; there was nothing in her empty gaze.

"Motherfucker," she muttered.

Then she pitched forward and passed out in his arms.

Job left his scooter in Yubei and flagged down a taxi and brought Ynez to his apartment. He carried her up three flights of stairs and into his room and lay her down upon his bedroll. Then he called the dispatch office and told them he wouldn't be coming in.

He called Cantey next and asked him if he knew how a person got off drugs. Cantey asked him what kind of drugs, and Job described Ynez's condition. Cantey told him he'd call him back, and fifteen minutes later, he did and said there wasn't much you could do other than drop the person off at a hospital or lock them in a room for a few days and hope for the best. Job assumed she was still there illegally and didn't know if anyone was looking for her or not, so he gave an elderly Kurdish man who lived next door some money to make sure she didn't leave, then went down to the corner market and bought some jugs of water and a few bottles of pain killers. He went to another store across the street and bought a large plastic bucket and a long extension cord. Then he returned to the apartment, where Ynez was still passed out.

He carefully took off her shoes and undressed her to her soiled underwear. He didn't want to violate her in any way, but he didn't want to leave her in the dirty briefs, either, so he averted his eyes when he removed them. Then he filled the bucket with warm water and gave her a sponge bath, cleaning off all the dried vomit and dirt and blood. Each additional thick scar he found on her back or upper arm or leg saddened and angered him, but there was nothing he could do about it, so he just grit his teeth and finished the job. Then he washed out the bucket and put it next to her in case she got sick again. Finally, he dressed her in a clean pair of his underwear and one of his T-shirts and bound her wrists and her ankles with the extension cord. She woke an hour later and saw the binds and saw him sitting on the other side of the unfurnished room, watching her.

"What the fuck is this?" she said.

"Nice to see you, too," he replied.

She squinted at him through bloodshot eyes, and he couldn't tell if she recognized him or not.

"Untie me."

"Not until you're off whatever you're taking—"

"Untie me, goddamn it!"

She fought against her restraints.

"You're not gonna tear those, so you might as well just wait it out," he said.

That only made her angrier, and she flopped across the floor and lashed out like an angry fish that had somehow gotten onto the deck of a ship, knocking over a lamp and a cardboard box that had been serving as a nightstand. She knocked over the bucket and sent it rolling across the room and fought and screamed and fought some more until she got tired, and then she lay there, breathing hard.

"The fuck do you want?" she asked.

"To help you," he said.

"Who asked you?"

"Ynez—"

"I don't want your help!" she screamed. Then she fought again until she finally wore herself out.

He sat with her for four days and four nights while she went through withdrawals. For the first two days, she fought like a hog-tied animal. She spent every waking moment struggling against her restraints until her wrists and ankles bled, and she kicked and screamed and bit and spat at him every time he got near. She shouted at him and swore at him and grunted at him and cursed him, and she cursed his mother and his father and God until she grew hoarse and then she cursed them all some more. She shat and pissed herself and threw up all over herself and all over the room, and she refused to let him clean her. She even fought during the rare moments she slept, railing in her dreams against unseen enemies and shivering so violently she seemed epileptic and grinding her teeth so hard that he thought she might break them.

On the third day, she finally began to stop fighting, exhausted from all the struggle and dehydrated from the diarrhea and vomiting and sweating. He convinced her to take a sip of water and some of the pain killers, and when she did, he thought for a brief moment that perhaps the worst had passed. Then she began to bargain with him. At first, it was bearable; she even referred to him by name and thanked him for taking her in. She spoke warmly and politely and told him that someone must have slipped her something where she worked and now that it had passed she was feeling much better and needed to get back. When he told her her work could wait a few more days, her face darkened and she swore at him and kicked over the plastic bucket and sent a slurry of urine and vomit across the floor. Before the bucket had even rolled to a stop, her facial muscles slackened and she apologized for the outburst. Her personality and moods were mercurial and changed in an instant, and she seemed as if she were possessed by demons.

After he cleaned up the mess, she apologized again and told him she was fine and just wanted to go home. He told her he'd let her go home in a couple of days; she told him it was no problem, that he shouldn't be bothering with her, but he said that it was no problem for him, either. Then she lashed out again and swore at him and kicked out at the bucket and toppled it over, but it was empty, and he carefully righted it and placed it just out of her reach.

They sat in silence for some time. Then she tried pleading with him once more. She swore she'd never touch drugs again. Then she offered him money, but he still wouldn't release her. She offered him sex after that; she said she was still a virgin and that she'd been waiting for him. He didn't reply, and then she said she wasn't actually a virgin and offered him things he hadn't even imagined in his most secret fantasies, things that made him blush or even made his stomach turn. Again, he said nothing, and that only further angered her; she asked him if he was a faggot and lashed out at him with a string of the foulest epithets he'd ever heard. He finally just got up and left the room because he couldn't stomach it anymore, and he stood there in the hallway for a while and tried not to cry as she lashed out at him for being a coward and a bastard and all sorts of other hurtful names.

He waited until she finally stopped shouting at him and then waited a few hours longer, and then he made some peanut butter sandwiches for her and some weak tea, but when he brought them into the room, he found her asleep. He sat with her through the night and gave her another sponge bath and cleaned and bandaged the wounds on her ankles and wrists and put on a fresh T-shirt and a pair of clean shorts. When she started to get the chills again, he wrapped her in blankets, and when she broke out in sweats, he gently wiped her brow with a wet towel.

On the fourth day, Ynez grew withdrawn. She stopped bargaining with him and stopped swearing at him and stopped drinking any water and refused the food and medications he offered. She sat all day staring out the window toward the craggy mountains in the far distance. At times, he sat there in silence as well; at other times, he tried striking up conversations with her, asking her what she'd been up to since they'd last met. Sometimes he'd just think out loud when she didn't answer him, telling her what he'd been up to in long, unbroken monologues. He also read sections of his grandfather's Bible to her, the Book of Matthew and the Book of Luke and some of the Psalms and Proverbs, too.

When he woke on the morning of the fifth day, he saw that she was already up. She asked him for some water, and he got her some. Then she told him she was ready to eat if that was all right with him. He made her a sandwich and undid the binds on her wrists so she could eat the sandwich herself.

After she was finished, she asked him for another sandwich. While she ate, she began to tell him about what had happened to her since they'd arrived in China. She'd made her way to Shanghai, where she'd found Daniel, but neither of them had been able to get into a university, so they began working in a microprocessor factory. After it closed, they heard about prospects in Shenzhen, but on their way there, some members of a nationalist movement took them off a train and forced themselves on her and beat Daniel so badly that his head swelled to the size of a watermelon. She'd managed to get him to a hospital, but a doctor there told her that Daniel was brain dead and that they'd be taking him off life support. She begged for them to reconsider, but they refused, and when she tried to fight them, she had to be removed from the hospital by four guards.

After Daniel was cremated by the state, and she was given no explanation of how to get his ashes or where they'd gone, she went to Shenzhen and found work in a factory that produced electric cars, but she kept getting sick from the solvents they used there. Then she got work at a satellite factory, but her manager kept forcing himself upon her, and when she refused his advances, he withheld her pay. She left the factory and made her way to Chongqing when a husband and wife promised her a hotel job there if she paid them two months' wages, but when she got to the city, there was no job and no hotel, and the husband and wife had disappeared. She found work as a waitress at a KTV parlor, but the money was hardly enough to live on, so she soon became a *zuotai xiaojie* and got paid to have drinks with the customers and applaud their karaoke and let them fondle her. A few weeks after starting the job, one of her clients pushed her into a restroom stall and raped her, and when she fought back, he slashed her face with a straight razor and beat her unconscious.

She began to get choked up and stopped there, saying that she was ashamed for what had become of her and that she was sorry she'd said what she'd said to him and had taken up his time. He told her not to be sorry and that he wasn't sorry and that finding her was the best thing that had happened to him since he'd left home. He showed her that he'd still had the now dog-eared and yellowed list of phrases she'd given him on the ship, and that he knew all of them by heart and that they'd helped him in his travels; he'd carried it everywhere he'd went, like the pieces of the advertisement from the magazine he'd fished out of the Willamette and had carried as a boy. She looked like she was going to cry again, so he went into the kitchen and made her another sandwich and got her a jug of water and some more of the pain medicine. Then he undid the binds on her ankles. He told her that he had to go back to work and that she could go if she wanted to or she could stay. Then, after a moment, he added that he wanted her to stay.

Job left her and took the subway out to Yubei. When he got there, he found his scooter miraculously still chained where he'd left it. He rode it back to the delivery service office downtown, and when Lee Jun Fan saw him, he grabbed him by the collar in front of everyone and started yelling at him. Job slapped away Lee Jun Fan's hand, and when Lee Jun Fan shoved him, Job pushed him to the ground. Everyone who was present stopped what they were doing and stared at Job in disbelief.

Job tossed the keys to the scooter onto a nearby table without waiting to see what Lee Jun Fan would do. Then he turned and left the office. Out on the street, he felt oddly calm and at peace. He'd found jobs before, he thought to himself, and he'd find jobs again.

He began to make his way back toward Americatown. At a wet market, he bought some carrots and potatoes. Then, after a moment, he added a small bunch of carnations to the purchase. Though he needed every yuan he had, the thought of brightening up his room for Ynez seemed well worth it.

After a few blocks, Job approached a large KTV parlor. Two attractive and heavily made-up Caucasian women in their late thirties approached the side employee entrance. He stopped and watched them for a moment as they disappeared through the thick steel doors.

For some reason, one of them made him think of his mother.

I remember the first time I saw a prostitute. I was in Salem with Eli and my grandpa and my grandpa's brother, Toe. I couldn't have been more than four or five years old. There were a few of them in an alley warming their hands over a fire. They were painted up like dolls and wore tight clothing or clothing you could see through or hardly any clothing at all. I thought they looked pretty; I didn't know who or what they were. My grandpa said nothing and just sort of pushed us along our way. Toe was much looser when it came to talking, whether people cared to hear what he had to offer or not. When he saw the women, he shook his head and spat in the dirt and said it's no wonder the world's such a hellhole. I don't remember much else of what Toe said anymore or anything about him or what he even looked like, but I still remember that, and it never sat right with me. It seemed like an easy thing to say, seeing as he had a strong back and a piece of land his father had given him. Who knows why those women were doing what they were doing, but my guess now is that they probably didn't have much of a choice. There are lots of things I've done to keep on going that I'm not so proud of, and I don't suppose I've done the last of it, either.

I think the important thing is to just keep on going.

V

Ynez said she'd stay only for the night, but then she stayed
for a second night, and then a third. Job fashioned a pillow
for her out of some towels, and he gave her his sleeping
bag and some yoga mats he'd found in a cardboard box
outside one of the luxury sky-rises. He slept on his old
bedroll on the other side of the room and lay awake at
night listening to her breathing, thinking back to the
weeks they'd spent in the sweltering hold of the *Hanne
Pernille*.

Through a friend of Cantey's, he got another job as a
courier for a delivery service near the airport. He had to
start at the bottom; there were no tips, and the schedule
was difficult, but the pay was decent. The work consisted
of delivering packages all over the city, things that were

too cheap or too difficult for the drones. Occasionally, he brought things to wealthy locals and expatriates who lived in the sky-rises and the gated lane homes and old renovated *siheyuan*. One day, he had to deliver something to the shoe factory he'd worked at; another time, he delivered something to Yongtong. While he stood at the entrance gate waiting for someone to sign for the package, he looked up at the factory where he'd spent so many similar evenings and watched the shadows of the workers moving behind the glowing windows. He wondered if any of them could see him standing there, and if so, if they were wishing they were outside as he'd wished when he'd been there.

After his shifts ended, he studied Chinese with Ynez or rode around the city looking for his mother at the brothels and KTV parlors and whorehouses. He bought a map and began to cross off blocks as he made his way through the city. He started with the upscale locations downtown, where the expensive Filipino and Russian women cost as much per hour as he earned in an entire month. He paid the cover charges and went inside the places that would allow him inside and looked for his mother among the lineups and among the *mami*s who oversaw the girls until they realized he wasn't actually interested in paying for sex and threw him out and forbade him from returning. At places he couldn't get into, he showed the photo of his mother to bouncers and doormen and waiters and said he had a large sum of money for her and he could pay them a finder's fee as well if they could lead him to her, but none of the men he spoke to were willing or able to help him. Money didn't seem to be an issue for them and they were protective of what seemed to be their property.

Near the end of the second week she stayed with him, Ynez started to get sick. She began sweating so much at night that it soaked her clothes and the sleeping bag and the yoga mats beneath it, and when Job touched her forehead, it felt like a warm radiator. Soon after that, she got the chills and began shaking so hard and chattering her teeth so badly he thought she might break them again, and he bundled her underneath blankets and clothing and towels, but she soon grew hot again and shucked it all off and got up and started pacing the room. Just before dawn one morning, she began vomiting. He brought her into the bathroom and held her hair behind her head as she threw up over and over until she had nothing left to give. Then she screamed and cursed and shouted until her voice went hoarse and then she racked with dry heaves. She finally passed out, and Job carried her back to his bedroom, where she slept fitfully until the following night.

The next day, Job asked one of the other couriers to cover his shift. Then he took Ynez to see a doctor at a free health clinic in Americatown. They arrived just before it opened; there were already a dozen people waiting outside. Among them was a pregnant teenager with pierced nostrils and eyebrows and crude facial tattoos. She wore torn and soiled jeans and a T-shirt that barely covered her swollen belly. An African mother and her scrawny child waited behind her; the boy's tiny arms were stick-thin, and his eyes were cloudy and red. There were also a few shifty young men covered with chancres and other telltale signs of syphilis. Standing at the center as if presiding over it all was a blind old Hispanic man with Parkinson's disease, who waved his dancing hands in the air as if he was conducting some silent and invisible orchestra. When Ynez saw them all gathered there like the attractions of a carnival sideshow, she started to turn away, but Job convinced her to stay.

Once it finally opened, they went inside and signed in under a fake name and waited. A Chinese news program aired on a television screen, broadcasting stories about rising inflation and the wars in Africa and immigration problems and childhood obesity; the air smelled of illness and disinfectant and sweat. More people streamed in until all of the seats were filled, and they continued to stream in until the floor was covered as well and there was nowhere left to stand. Just before noon, a nurse with a clipboard entered from a hallway and read the bogus name Ynez had given her off the list. Ynez turned to Job.

"You want me to go with you?" he said.

"You don't have to," she said.

"I know I don't have to."

The nurse called the name again, and they got up and followed her down the hallway. She led them to an empty examination room; yellowing eye charts and old nervous system diagrams curled from the walls. The cheap, steel cabinets were locked, and a small and overflowing red medical waste container stood near the door.

"Wait in here," said the nurse.

She left the room. Job stayed by the door, and Ynez sat in a chair, nervously scratching her arms. Neither spoke. After twenty minutes, a tired-looking doctor of mixed Asian and Caucasian race entered the room; his green scrubs were stained and wrinkled, and his eyes were bloodshot, but his smile seemed genuine. He asked why they were there, and Ynez told him, and he began to ask her a long list of questions. She replied to most of them with nods or by shaking her head. Then he asked her how long she'd been using drugs. Job offered to leave the room, but before he could finish, Ynez interrupted him and told the doctor while still looking at Job that she'd been using midazolam and fentanyl and methamphetamine and anything else that she could get her hands on for almost a year. The doctor then went on to ask her how many sexual partners she'd had, and while still looking at Job, she responded by saying that she couldn't remember or accurately put a number on it, but if she had to guess, she'd put the figure at fifty, if not more.

"Still sure you want me?" she bluntly asked Job, as if they were the only two people in the room.

He nodded and said the same thing she'd said to him in the hold of the *Hanne Pernille*—that he saw so much more in her than that—and she turned away, fighting the urge to cry. The doctor examined her and recommended she get tested for STDs. Before he left the room, he also suggested she stay off drugs and look for another line of work. He said he saw hundreds of girls like her every month and that the ones who didn't change their lifestyles were usually dead within a year.

After the doctor left, the nurse returned and took blood samples. She told them they could wait for the results and then left the room. As soon as they were alone again, Ynez turned to Job.

"You can go now if you want," she said.

"It's all right," he said. "My shift's covered, anyway."

Ten minutes passed. Then twenty minutes, and then thirty. Ynez began to pace; Job studied the circuitry of the human nervous system on a wall poster and followed the path of nerves down the arm from the musculocutaneous to the radial to the median to the ulnar. It all seemed so fragile and so delicate, and it reminded him of the barren trees during winter back home. After forty-five minutes, he offered to go to the nurses' station and get an update, but before Ynez could reply, the nurse returned, carrying a folder full of paperwork.

"You're a lucky young woman," she said.

Ynez's HIV test had come up negative. So had her tests for syphilis and hepatitis and TB. She did have a bad infection, but it was treatable with strong antibiotics. Given what was going around among the prostitutes and

intravenous drug users of Chongqing, the nurse said the
fact that she hadn't contracted any other diseases was
nothing short of a miracle.

Ynez instinctively reached out and embraced Job,
finally allowing herself to cry. He held her tightly in his
arms, fighting back tears of his own.

Job returned to work and picked up some extra shifts to
cover the time he'd missed. When he wasn't working, he
studied Chinese with Ynez or continued searching for his
mother. He finished checking all the downtown brothels
and KTV parlors and began to look for her in
Huangjueping. He didn't see her at any of them and no
one he'd spoken to had seen or heard of her, either, and he
spent much of his remaining savings on entrance fees and
cover charges and gasoline.

After he crossed the last block of Huangjueping off
his map, he began to look for his mother in the district of
Shapingba. The area stood between the Jialing River and
the Gele Mountains and was full of stadiums and
universities and factories and was grittier and more run-
down than Yuzhong and Jiangbei. The establishments
there were grittier and more run-down as well, and most
of the women who worked in them were Americans or
Hispanics or Eastern Europeans. The cover charges and
entrance fees cost less, but there were more locations to
investigate and more women at each location, and he soon

began to run out of money. At one of the brothels, he met a Hispanic woman with cracked teeth and severely pocked skin who said through a translator that she recognized his mother from his photograph, but the more questions he asked her, the more he began to realize that the woman was delusional or even insane. The woman then went on to say that she herself was Job's mother and that his name was Jesús and that she'd been looking for him for years. She laughed as he made his way to the exit, and he continued to hear her shrill laughter in his thoughts long after he'd left.

He finished searching the brothels of Xiyong and began to make his way through Chenjiaqiao. He went into all the establishments he could and looked over one lineup after another, but he saw no one who looked even remotely like his mother. At the ones he couldn't get into or didn't want to squander his money on the entrance fees, he showed the photograph of his mother to the bouncers or doormen or anyone else he could catch outside, but none of them recognized her, either. As he made his way back to his scooter after yet another fruitless query, a Caucasian man in a sharkskin suit approached him. The man sucked on a vape pen and walked with a limp and reeked of rice wine and strong cologne; his hair was dyed the color of plums, and his teeth were so white and even that Job assumed they were false.

"I know woman you are looking for," said the man, speaking with a thick Czech accent.

"What woman?"

"The woman in photograph. She goes by name Desire, but is not her real name."

"Where is she?"

"What's it worth to you?"

Job hesitated.

"I'm entrepreneur, not social worker," said the man. "You want charity, put out hat."

"I'll give you a hundred yuan," said Job.

The man laughed.

"You see those women?" he said, pointing to a trio of Caucasian prostitutes waiting by a nearby street corner. "They make me a hundred yuan every ten minutes. Each."

"I'll give you two hundred, then."

"Make it thousand."

"I want to see her first."

"No way."

"You want the money, show me where she is."

The man hesitated, and Job turned away and started to unlock his scooter.

"All right, all right," said the man, following Job. "You give me five hundred now, I show you where she is."

The man then held out his hand, and Job paid him. Then the man turned and limped off toward a less-populated side street. Job locked up his scooter and followed the man, who told him his name was Jaro. They walked east for a few blocks and then turned onto another side street, where there were even fewer people out and fewer open businesses. An uneasy feeling began to grow in the pit of Job's stomach.

"Where are you taking me?" he said.

"Is just a little farther," said Jaro.

They went two more blocks before Jaro stopped outside a dilapidated apartment building. He pressed a button on a panel near the door and said a few words in Czech over an intercom, and after a moment, a buzzer sounded and the door unlocked. Jaro went to open the door, but Job stopped him.

"I can take it from here," he said.

Jaro hesitated.

"Just tell me where she is, or I'm not giving you the second half," said Job.

"Okay," said Jaro. "She is on seventh floor. Room 316."

Job left Jaro outside and entered the building. He approached an elevator and pressed a button, but no elevator came. After a few minutes, he found a stairwell, and when he finally reached the third floor, he stepped out into a garbage-strewn hallway. The walls were tagged with graffiti in a profusion of languages, and a few overhead bulbs illuminated the space with a weak and uneven light.

He made his way down the hall until he reached a room with no number on the door, but it stood between rooms with the numbers 315 and 317. He pressed a buzzer next to the door and waited, but no one answered. He pressed the buzzer again, and still no one answered. He pounded on the door with his fist. Finally, he heard shuffling footsteps on the other side of the door followed by the sound of a chain unlocking. Then the door opened to reveal a three-hundred-pound Slavic woman wearing a stained and fraying slip that looked like it'd been fashioned from a tent. Her eyes were wild and her hair was a ratty nest, and she had a crude and faded tattoo of a dagger and rose atop one of her swollen bosoms. A TV blared in one corner of the room, and a stained and caved-in mattress lay on the floor next to the wall.

The woman grinned and said something to Job in a language he couldn't understand, though it was clear that it meant something lascivious. Her breath stank of vodka and mushrooms and death, and he recoiled from it and stumbled backward into the hallway. She called after him, greedily licking her lips.

"Sorry," he said.

Her eyes darkened and she stumbled out into the hallway, railing curses at him in some thick Slavic tongue. Job tripped over some empty bottles and ran toward the stairwell, and she shouted after him as he went. He hurried down the stairs, leaping them two and three at a time. When he got to the lobby, he flung open the door and went outside, but Jaro was nowhere to be seen.

He returned to the street where he'd met Jaro and approached the prostitutes. When he asked them about

Jaro, they looked at him with confused and vacant
expressions, saying they didn't work for Jaro or anyone, or
have any idea who Job was talking about.

Weeks passed, and the seasons began to change. The
suffocating humidity of the summer returned to the city,
and the monsoon rains came and flooded its streets. The
waters coursed down the hilly areas and ran along the
curbs and gutters, depositing the city's trash into its
murky rivers. Once swept up into its currents, it all floated
downstream toward the unseen and faraway ocean,
bobbing and tilting like the flotsam of some vast and
immeasurable wreck.

It took Job longer to get around the city, so he had to
spend more time on his deliveries. With the little time he
had to himself, he continued to search for his mother and
was soon able to cross Tuzhu and Zhongliang off his
slowly shrinking map. He ran out of money at one point
after spending it all on cover charges and gasoline and
was forced to put his search on hold, but as soon as he got
paid again, he resumed looking for her in Qingmuguan
and then in Zengjia.

He took every extra shift he could get. One of the
other couriers left for a better job, one broke his hip and
leg in an accident, and another was deported, so there
were plenty available. By the end of the summer, he was
one of the longest-tenured couriers at the delivery service

and was given many of the easier routes. He was also given one of the newer scooters that had belonged to one of the other couriers who'd left and was able to get around faster and didn't have to spend so much money on fuel.

He worked all day every day and he continued to look for his mother every night. Ynez ended up finding work as a maid in a hotel and was often gone by the time he got back, and he usually left before she returned. They saw little of each other, but he knew she was still staying there from the maid uniforms she hung out the window to dry or the orange peels she left in the trash. After a couple of weeks, she left him an envelope from the hotel she was working at with some money in it, but he wouldn't take it. A couple of weeks after that, she left him another envelope, but he also left it untouched.

After he finished looking for his mother in Zengjia, Job began searching for her in Huilongba. Once he was finished checking all the brothels and KTV parlors and whorehouses in Huilongba, he started looking in Bafu. While watching a lineup at the club of a seedy hotel near the industrial park, he saw a woman walking toward one of the back karaoke rooms who looked vaguely like his mother. He pushed his way past a bartender and followed the woman into a back room, but when she turned around, he saw that she had yellow-green eyes and a hatchet nose and was clearly someone else. The bartender rushed into the room with a bouncer and they shoved Job face first into a wall, opening a gash above his right eye.

Then they dragged him toward the exit and tossed him out into the street.

He made his way back to his scooter and rode home. Blood seeped into his eye from the gash and made it difficult to see. After he finally got back to his building, he locked his scooter and went inside. Ynez was awake and her hair was wet from showering, and she was ironing her outfit on the back of an old padded board. She immediately stopped what she was doing when she saw him.

"Oh my God," she said, approaching him. "What happened?"

"It's nothing," he said.

She dabbed at the wound with a hand towel, but it only bled even more.

"It's fine," he said, pulling away.

"Hang on a sec."

She got a needle and thread.

"Really, it's nothing—"

He tried to pull away again, but she stopped him.

"Let me," she said.

Before he could reply, she threaded the needle and then dabbed at the wound with some cheap spirits. Then she pushed the needle into his skin near the end of the gash and pushed it through the other side. He grimaced from the pain.

"Hold still," she said.

She pushed the needle through his skin again and pulled it out on the other side of the wound. He watched her as she worked; her face was close to his and he could smell the soap on her freshly washed skin and he could smell oranges on her breath. He traced the lines of her scars with her eyes, and she noticed him staring.

"What?" she asked.

He didn't say anything, and she grew self-conscious and turned away from him.

"I know," she said. "I look like a freak show."

"No, you don't," he said. "You're beautiful."

"You're an idiot—"

Before she could finish, he leaned forward and kissed her. She hesitated, but after a brief moment, she couldn't help but kiss him back. They tore off each other's clothing and moved to the floor, and as soon as they were on the sleeping bag, they began to make love.

The humidity finally broke in September and the monsoon rains came to an end, but the thick gray fog that shrouded Chongqing every spring and every autumn soon returned and made it difficult to see farther than a block. Another courier left the delivery service without warning, and another new courier was hired. Job's scooter broke down one day and he had to push it all the way back to the service center. Another day, he was stopped by police and threatened with arrest for not having the proper documents, but he was able to get off by giving the officers his money. Some immigrants got lucky in certain situations while others did not; to a casual observer, justice may have seemed like a cruel and impartial game of chance, with severe and often irrevocable outcomes.

He continued to look for his mother and eventually crossed Bafu off his map as well as parts of Jiulongpo. Since beginning his search, he'd crossed off more than half the towns in the districts of Yuzhong and Shapingba, but he knew his progress was far from certain. In the six months he'd been looking for her, she might have moved from one location to another or moved to another city, or worse, and that was assuming that she was even working in a brothel or KTV parlor in Chongqing at all.

He finished making his way through Baishiyi and then began searching in Hangu. He soon ran out of money again and thought about taking some of the cash Ynez had left him, but he left it alone, wanting to give her every reason to stay. He took extra shifts and worked nights and offered to do the deliveries of the other couriers bound for Hangu or Xipeng or any of the other towns in the Jiulongpo district. In between deliveries, he began to check more brothels and KTV parlors and whorehouses off his list. It was a slower way to work, but any progress he made was better than no progress at all.

After a while, he was able to cross Hangu and Xipeng off his map as well and then began to look for his mother in Shiqiao. One day while delivering a package to a factory office in Dadukou, Job saw a woman who looked vaguely familiar tearing the cellophane wrapper off a package of cigarettes after leaving a corner market. He swung the scooter around at the next intersection and made a U-turn and began to follow the woman from a distance. From behind, it was impossible to tell if it was actually his mother; he had few memories of her, other than from the stories his brother and grandfather had told him. He had little idea what she looked like when she was walking or smoking or moving or even at rest. The woman seemed to be about the same height as his mother and of a similar build, but her hair was different from the way it had looked in the photograph; it was shorter and dyed the color of rust. The woman also had full sleeves of faded irezumi tattoos on both arms. Colorful dragons and serpents and tigers crawled up from her wrists and disappeared writhing beneath the arms of her tight-fitting qipao.

When the woman reached the end of the block, she turned onto a narrow side street. Job followed her; the traffic on the side street was at a standstill, and he had to weave through cars and other scooters and bicycles to keep pace. Before long, he could feel his cell phone vibrating in his pocket. He pulled it out and glanced at the display, and he saw that it was the dispatcher calling him about another delivery, but he didn't answer it and shut it off before putting it away.

He approached a wall of stopped vehicles and people at the next intersection and was forced to stop himself as well. He watched helplessly as the woman crossed the street just ahead of the light change and disappeared into the crowded sidewalk on the other side. He shoved his way forward through the mob and pushed people aside and then accelerated out into the intersection. A taxi honked and swerved to avoid hitting him, and a bus coming from the other direction blasted its horn at him and missed him by a matter of inches.

As soon as he was across the street, he resumed following the woman. Before long, he hit another wall of traffic. He jumped the curb and raced the scooter up onto the sidewalk and weaved through the crowd honking and shouting at the pedestrians in his way.

Once he made it past the standstill, he rode off the curb and back onto the street. The woman turned again at the next intersection, and Job continued to follow her. Halfway up the block, she approached the entrance to a seedy-looking KTV parlor called Golden Sunrises. He gunned the scooter and pulled up to a service entrance on the side of the building. Then he craned his neck to get a glimpse of the woman as she went inside.

Even though he was fifty feet away, and even though she looked little like he'd remembered, when she turned back and looked past and through him—tilting her head slightly and brushing aside her hair—he saw her fine-boned face and her gold-flecked green eyes, and he knew instinctively and without a doubt that it was his mother.

Job brought the package to the factory office in Dadukou and finished his shift. Then he went back to the KTV parlor where he'd seen his mother. A number of foreign businessmen wearing bespoke suits were making their way inside, while a group of wealthy Chinese students came drunkenly stumbling out. At night and lit up, the place looked far more exotic and upscale than it did during the day.

He locked up his scooter and followed the businessmen inside. A dozen Caucasian hostesses lined up by the door bowed to the group as they entered; two burly Asian bouncers sat chatting on stools near the door. The lobby of the parlor was cavernous and dark, and it smelled like perfume and disinfectant and smoke. The walls were draped with purple and black curtains even though there were no windows anywhere, and a few fluorescent lights bathed the area with a warm red glow.

Job watched as a hostess ushered the group of businessmen toward one of the private rooms in back. As soon as his eyes adjusted to the light, he saw a counter where a harsh-looking older woman ran a credit card through a reader. He peeled off from the group and began to make his way toward the counter. On the other side of the room, a bartender poured drinks for a few groups of men. Some were Chinese and some were foreigners; some wore wedding bands and some did not. Some looked affluent and some appeared to be working class. A wall of mirrored shelves stood behind the bartender, filled with glittering bottles of rice wine and sake and single-malt scotch.

After the woman finished processing the bill, she looked to Job. A staticky voice crackled over a walkie-talkie clipped to her belt.

"I'm looking for this woman," said Job, showing her the photograph of his mother. "You know where I can find her?"

The woman shook her head.

"I saw her come in here."

"Sorry," said the woman, turning back to her work.

"Her name's Merab Hammon," said Job.

Someone spoke behind him.

"Is there a problem?"

Job turned to see a tall and wiry Filipino floor manager. He wore black slacks, pointed black shoes, and a black dress shirt, and his inky hair was slicked back over his almond-shaped skull. He moved silently and gracefully across the room like a shark fin cutting through water. When he approached, Job could make out a nametag on the breast of his suitcoat that read "SAENSAK."

"I'm looking for this woman," said Job, showing Saensak the photograph.

Saensak didn't even glance at it.

"Never seen her," he said.

"But I saw her come in here—"

Saensak interrupted him.

"You saw wrong," he said.

"She's my mother—"

Before Job could finish, Saensak rammed some sort of blackjack Taser into Job's solar plexus. He'd pulled it out so fast that it had seemed to materialize out of nowhere, and it disappeared just as quickly back to wherever it had come from.

"Get lost," said Saensak.

Job dropped to a knee, tingling and sucking for air. As soon as he got his breath back, he stood up, but instead of heading toward the exit, he remained where he was.

"Please," he said, wheezing.

"Are you deaf?"

"I really need to speak to her—"

Before Job could finish, Saensak rammed the device into Job's rib cage again. Job felt one of his ribs crack, and he dropped to a knee.

"Don't let me catch you in here again," said Saensak. "You understand?"

Without waiting for a reply, Saensak turned and nodded to the two bouncers, and they came over and yanked Job to his feet. Then they carried him toward a service door. When they reached it, one of them flung it open, and the other shoved Job down a short flight of steps.

He landed on the hard pavement in a puddle full of vomit and grease.

Job returned to his apartment and stripped out of his soiled clothing. He could see his reflection in the bathroom mirror and saw two large bruises on his torso. One was in the center of his chest, shaped like a fist and almost black in color; the other was mottled and purplish and spread across his rib cage like a wine stain. Both hurt when he touched them, and it hurt incredibly whenever he inhaled.

He had to go the bathroom, but he had pain when he tried to go standing up, so he sat down. As soon as he finished urinating, he looked into the water in the toilet bowl underneath him and saw that it was red. He flushed the toilet and got up again and took a long hot shower. Then he dried off and began to put on some clean clothes. He called Ynez, but it went straight to her voicemail, so he left a short message, telling her that he'd be home when he could.

He went back to Taojia, where he found an unoccupied bench at a bus stop across from Golden Sunrises and watched its entrance. After a while, a group of well-dressed Chinese men left through the main lobby and got into a waiting sedan, and a while after that, a few inebriated Westerners left with some *xiaojie*. A short time later, another group of women and some of the *mami*s who managed them left through the service entrance on the side of the building, but his mother wasn't among them. Job continued to wait. He started to get tired, so he bought a can of coffee from one of the nearby convenience stores that were open all night. Then he returned to the bench and watched another group of businessmen leave Golden Sunrises with a few more *xiaojie*. Not long after that, he watched one of the bouncers leave through the service entrance, then saw a few more customers go and watched some migrant janitors and cleaning women arrive.

Job began to get tired again, so he bought another can of coffee. While he sat there drinking it and continuing to watch the entrances, he thought about what he'd say to his mother, but he couldn't even think of where or how to begin. Just before dawn, another group of Chinese businessmen left through the entrance to the main lobby of the parlor, and a few minutes later, Job saw the woman he thought was his mother exit through the service entrance on the side of the building. He got up and hurried across the street and approached her.

"Mom," he said.

She didn't respond nor even react to his voice, so he called to her once more.

"Merab Hammon," he said.

Again, she didn't respond. He caught up to her and grabbed her arm.

"Wait," he said.

She stopped and turned to face him. Her pupils were dilated, and he could see track marks running up and down both arms despite the full sleeves of tattoos.

"Don't you recognize me?" he said.

The woman didn't respond. He looked to her eyes for surprise or recognition or even avoidance, but he saw nothing; they were as empty as the eyes of a doll.

"It's me," he said. "Job."

"Sorry," she said.

She turned and started to walk off.

"Hang on," he said.

He grabbed her arm again, but she yanked it free.

"Fuck off."

"Please—"

She interrupted him.

"You want some money?" she said. "Here. Now go."

She dropped some coins at his feet, but before he could reply, he heard a voice behind him.

"The fuck?"

Job turned to see Saensak approaching from the service entrance.

"I told you not to come back here," he said.

"This isn't your concern," said Job.

"The hell it's not—"

Before Saensak could finish, Job head-butted him in the face and broke his nose with a dull and sickening crunch. Saensak raised a hand to his face and looked to Job with a mixture of surprise and rage, but before he could decide what to do, Job kneed him in the groin as hard as he could, and Saensak went down, groaning. Someone shouted from over by the service entrance, and Job looked back and saw one of the club's bouncers exiting the building. He turned and ran after the woman, and the bouncer chased him. Another bouncer exited through the service entrance and approached Saensak, then ran after the others.

Job shouted toward the woman.

"Wait," he said. "I just want to talk to you."

Before Job could catch up to the woman, the first bouncer tackled him, and they crashed to the pavement in a heap. Then they began pummeling each other, but the bouncer was too big and strong, and he quickly flipped Job onto his back. He tore into Job's rib cage with a series of jabs and hooks; Job pinched down his arms, and the man punched him hard across the face with a solid right. Job turned his head and caught a glimpse of the woman looking back at him as she continued to walk away from the scene. For the briefest of moments, he saw what he thought was a faint glimmer of recognition in her eyes, but then he heard footsteps and approaching voices. When he turned back to see what it was, he saw Saensak's shoe come speeding toward his face, and after it hit him, everything went black.

He dreamed he was back in Ellendale, and that he was sitting before a large fire in the center of the village. Everyone he knew was gathered around it; Ynez was there, and Eli was there, and so was their grandfather. Jayel was there, too, and Old Lady Simons, and the girl with Down syndrome. There were others there as well who weren't from his village, people like Sister Vy and Vargas and the women from Salem, but as it was a dream, it didn't seem strange to him that the dead and the living and those from his past and present all mingled together. There was no animosity between the various parties, and it felt like a celebration was taking place. After a while, people began to bring out platters of food and jugs of wine and spits with roasted animals on them, and at the end of the group bearing food was his mother. When her eyes met with his, she smiled warmly.

When he woke, Job found himself lying on a bare mattress inside a cramped and darkened jail cell. His skull throbbed, his right eye was swollen shut, and his entire right side hurt as if he'd been hit by a car. He moved his tongue around his dry and bile-tasting mouth, and he felt a few gaps where a couple of his teeth had been. He raised his right hand to touch his face and realized that his right pinky and ring finger were broken and would not budge, despite great efforts to move them.

He tried to yell for someone to come, but all he could muster was a weak croak. He struggled to a sitting position and took in his surroundings with his good eye;

the room was about eight by ten feet wide and had no windows, and the mattress he sat on was stained with urine and sweat and blood. A fetid and stinking bucket stood in one corner of the cell, but he didn't remember using it and assumed its contents had been left by the cell's previous occupant. He got up and struggled his way toward a thick steel door; the laces from his boots were gone, and his feet slipped in his shoes. Halfway across the cell, the floor tilted beneath his feet and he had to pause and reach for the wall before he was able to continue. When he finally got to the door, he tried to yell again, but he couldn't manage more than a groan.

Job struggled to make a fist with his left hand and then pounded against the door until his fist throbbed, but it hardly made any noise, and no one came. He made his way back to the bed and sat down. Then he waited. After an hour, a small horizontal slot at the base of the door opened and a tray of watery rice was shoved into the cell and the slot closed again. Half of the rice ended up on the floor and there was something moving in the half remaining on the tray. He got up and approached it, and when he bent over to look, he saw a thumb-sized cockroach flopping around in the thin gruel.

He left the tray on the floor and went back to the bed again. Then he closed his eyes and tried to sleep. He lay there for hours but could not fall asleep, so he finally just opened his eyes again and began counting the spots of black mildew that speckled the ceiling and walls.

When he reached a count of a thousand, he started all over again.

A week passed. The first few days, Job shouted and knocked against the door, but no one came and he heard nothing, and he eventually stopped wasting his energy. Each day, another tray of watery rice was shoved into his cell, and each day, the slot opened up again and stayed open until he shoved the tray back through. His ribs stopped hurting after a few days and he was able to breathe deeply again, and the swelling around his eye went down a few days after that and he was again able to see out of both eyes.

On the eighth day, he woke to the sound of the door being unlocked. The bright light of the outside hall hurt his eyes and caused him to squint. When he finally adjusted to the light, he saw two armed guards standing outside. They told him in Chinese to get up, and he struggled to his feet and followed them into the hallway. They led him through a locked door and down another hallway and through another locked door, and then they shoved him into a small visitation room. When he saw the woman he believed was his mother sitting on the other side of a thick glass panel, his heart began to hammer in his chest.

The guards exited the room, and he went forward and sat down. The woman picked up the phone on her side, and he picked up the phone on his.

"You shouldn't have come here," she said.

His throat tightened.

"I knew it was you—"

She interrupted him.

"You're lucky the police showed up," she said. "What were you thinking?"

"I had to find you."

"You should've stayed home."

"There's nothing there."

"What about your brother?"

He shook his head. Her lack of a reaction to the news felt worse to him than a punch in the gut.

"You shouldn't have come looking for me," she said. "You were better off thinking I was dead. Both of us were."

"Don't say that."

"It's true," she said. "I'm not the person you think I am anymore. Probably never was."

"Mom—"

"Goddamn it, don't call me that," she snapped, choking up. He didn't reply, choking up as well. The door behind Job opened and the guards returned, and one of them told his mother to hurry up.

"I pulled some strings to get you out of here," she said. "Don't thank me, because it's more for my sake than it is yours. I also left some money for you so you can do something with your life."

"Please—"

She interrupted him again.

"Don't try and find me again," she said. "And don't go back to the club, either. Saensak will kill you."

"Wait—"

She hung up before he could reply and then stood and turned to leave.

"Mom!" he shouted, standing up.

Again, she didn't reply. He watched her disappear through the exit and then stood there until the guards finally took him away.

The following day, Job was released. No one gave him an explanation or any instructions or a warning. He was simply taken from his cell to processing, and at processing, he was given back his phone and his wallet and his shoelaces. He was also given a sealed envelope that had no writing on it and a small plastic bag containing two of his teeth.

Two guards led him out to the prison gates, and the gates opened and he went through them. He glanced around the area surrounding the prison and saw the Yuxing Cell Factory and the Shengdi Semiconductor Plant and the Chongqing Jiangbei International Airport and recognized the part of the city he was in. Then he turned around and looked back at the prison. It was enormous and sterile and surrounded with a high fence crowned with razor wire, and it looked no different than any of the other buildings in the area, most of which were clothing and electronics factories.

As he made his way toward the nearest subway station, he opened the padded envelope. Inside the envelope, he found three banded stacks of hundred-yuan notes. It was more money than he'd ever seen in his lifetime and he got nervous that someone might see it. He stuffed the bills into his pockets and threw away the envelope in a nearby trash can. Then he checked his cell phone; there had been sixteen missed calls during the time he was locked up, and all but one of them had come from Ynez.

Job tried calling her back, but she didn't answer. He thought about leaving her a message, but he couldn't think of how to explain things to her, so he didn't leave one. He took the subway back toward Americatown and went back to his apartment, but there was no one there. He showered and put on some clean clothes and ate a quick dinner of cold noodles and instant coffee. Then he got his penny knife from his things and hid it in his boot where he could easily reach it.

He left the apartment and made his way back to Taojia. The bench at the bus stop across the street from Golden Sunrises was occupied, so he found an alley and watched the entrance to the KTV parlor from there. He watched groups of foreign businessmen and wealthy Chinese come and go, and he watched dozens of *xiaojie* come alone or in groups and then go alone or with customers. He watched the sun rise in the east over the Wushan Mountains and slowly bleed into the smog-choked sky, too, but during all this time, he didn't see his mother leave nor arrive.

He watched more groups of foreign businessmen and wealthy Chinese come and go, and he watched more *xiaojie* arrive and leave. At one point, his phone rang and it was Ynez, but he didn't know what to say to her or how to say it, so he just let it go to voicemail.

Just after dawn, he saw the older Chinese woman who worked at the front counter of the parlor leaving through the service entrance. He jogged across the street and approached her.

"Excuse me," he said.

The woman ignored him, but he grabbed her arm and addressed her in Chinese.

"I'm looking for my mother," he said, showing her the photograph.

She shook her head.

"Please," he said. "I know you know her."

She pulled her arm free and hurried off. He glanced back toward the service entrance to the KTV parlor, and after a moment, he saw another *xiaojie* leaving.

Job made his way over to the service entrance and waited in the shadows. When another *xiaojie* exited

243

through the side door, he emerged from where he was hiding and went inside. He wandered through the back hallways of the KTV parlor; dark and narrow, they smelled like hair spray and semen and cigarette smoke. He looked into each room as he went past them; some had large leather couches and big flat-screen televisions and glass tables covered with empty bottles and picked-over dishes of fruit. A maid cleaned away the debris in one room; another room looked like a dressing area and had chairs and tables with scratched-up vanity mirrors and racks of shiny short evening gowns and sleeveless tops and miniskirts. A young *xiaojie* was there, changing into jeans and a pink sweatshirt; her cell phone rang and played a few bars of some saccharine pop song before she answered it and spoke rapidly in some Slavic language he couldn't understand.

Job rounded a corner and thought he saw Saensak going into an office at the other end of the hallway. He slowly made his way down the hallway and entered the office, but when he got there, he found it empty. Before he could figure out where Saensak had gone, Saensak emerged soundlessly from the hallway behind him and smashed him in the kidneys with his blackjack. Job dropped to a knee and sucked for air, and Saensak frisked him and found the money.

"Well, well," he said.

Job reached for the money, but Saensak stepped aside and shoved him to the floor.

"You animals never learn," he said, kicking the door closed behind him and stuffing the money into his pocket. "You spend all of your time chasing after things that you can never have."

"Where is she?" said Job.

"Who knows? Chengdu? Mianyang? I would've asked you the same thing, but it's obvious now that you don't know the answer, either."

"You son of a bitch—"

Saensak kicked him in the ribs.

"You ruined a good revenue stream of mine, and now you're going to pay for it with your life," he said.

Job struggled to his feet and lunged for Saensak, but Saensak sidestepped him and smashed him in the gut again with the blackjack as he went stumbling past. Job bumped into a desk and sent a picture frame and stack of papers and a glass paperweight careening to the floor. Then he crashed into the wall and fell to a knee again, clutching his side and sucking for air.

"Time to die," said Saensak.

He smashed Job over the head with the blackjack and laid him out on the floor. Job saw stars again and tasted his own coppery blood in his throat. He struggled to his knees, but Saensak kicked him in the ribs again, and after he went down, Saensak kicked him in the face and then once more in the side, and he felt another one of his ribs break. The thought occurred to Job that he was going to die there on the floor in Saensak's office. Then he looked over and saw his distorted reflection in the glass of the paperweight. He reached over for it and managed to get a hold of it, then turned and heaved it at Saensak. It hit Saensak squarely in the chest with a dull thump, and Saensak dropped the blackjack and staggered backward.

Job scrambled to his feet and tackled Saensak at the waist. They knocked over the desk and went crashing to the floor. The two rolled across the room, swinging wildly at each other and straining for purchase; Job got in a few shots to Saensak's body, but Saensak was bigger and stronger, and he managed to flip Job over and onto his back. Then he punched Job across the mouth with a hard right, and Job's head snapped backward and cracked against the floor.

The world grew blurry and appeared to be on fire in Job's peripheral vision. He saw two or three of everything, as if he was looking through a kaleidoscope. Before he could get his bearings, Saensak grabbed him by the throat and began to squeeze. He started to choke and swatted at Saensak's face, but Saensak only ended up squeezing even harder, and Job began to asphyxiate. Things started to go black, but then he remembered his penny knife. He reached down for his boot and fished it out, then swung it up with every last bit of energy he could summon and drove it as hard as he could into Saensak's side again and again until Saensak finally released him.

Job scrambled out from underneath Saensak and began to gasp for air. Then he glanced down at Saensak.

Saensak coughed up a bubbling mouthful of bright red blood as he looked up in disbelief. He backed up against the wall and tried to struggle to his feet, but only got a few inches off the ground before sliding back down again.

"Well," he croaked, then he coughed up another mouthful of blood. "Well."

Job reached into Saensak's pockets and took back his money. Saensak lazily swatted at him, but Job slapped Saensak's hand away. He hesitated for a moment, as if he was thinking of something to say, but he ended up saying nothing at all.

Then he turned and slowly staggered out of the room.

He made his way back toward the service entrance and left the KTV parlor, avoiding the security cameras as best as he could and staying close to the walls and shadows. As he stumbled off, he took in air in short and painful breaths. Every step he took, felt like he was being stabbed in the ribs, and his entire torso felt like it was on fire.

He set out for the subway and kept off the main streets. Each time he heard a siren, he thought it was coming for him. He soon grew lightheaded, and his knees began to buckle beneath him. Halfway to the station, he had to stop to rest because the pain was so great. He went into a park and sat down on a bench, and he must have passed out, because when he woke, it was late afternoon and his mouth was dry and the sun was beginning to go down behind the thick veil of smog hanging above the city.

He struggled the rest of the way to the subway station and then got on an empty car and rode it back to Americatown. When he reached his stop, he got off the train and made his way toward the exit. It took him twenty minutes to make it up the stairs, and when he finally got to the top of them, his clothes were soaked with sweat. When he stepped out onto the street, he was surprised to see that it was already nighttime again.

He gritted his teeth and struggled his way back to his apartment building. At one point, he started to cough up blood, and he had to lean against a wall until he could gather himself enough to continue. He eventually turned onto the block his apartment building was on and saw a light on in the window of the apartment above his, but he had to stop again because the pain was so great. He took a few more steps but then stumbled and took a knee. He began to cough up more blood, and when he finished coughing, he tried to get back up again, but he could not.

Then he sat down against the wall for a moment and closed his eyes and listened to the sounds of the city and the sound of his own breathing and the faint sirens in the distance.

He didn't remember passing out again, and when he woke some hours later, he saw Ynez's scarred face surrounded by the hazy glow of a sodium arc streetlamp.

"I've been looking all over for you," she said.

For a moment, he thought he might be dreaming, or that he might be dead and in heaven, but then he tried to sit up and he felt the sharp and stabbing pain of his broken ribs again.

"What happened?" she asked.

His throat tightened, and he felt a lump beginning to form in it. There was so much he wanted to say, but he could not think of what to say first or how to say it, and when he opened his mouth to speak, all he could manage to utter was a weak and raspy croak.

She reached under his arms and helped pull him to his feet.

"Come on," she said. "Let's get you inside."

There's this dream I have every now and then. In the dream, I'm sixteen again, and I'm on the train from Dongguan to Chongqing. There's an old Chinese man sitting next to me, and he's telling me a story. I think this man told me this story in real life back then, but I can't remember. All my dreams and memories eventually end up bleeding together. Anyway, the story he's telling me is about this frog in a shallow well. This frog tells some turtle that comes along that he's so happy 'cause he gets to jump about the railing 'round the mouth of the well, and he gets rest in the holes in the wall of the well, and if he jumps in the water, it only comes up to his armpits, and if he walks in the mud, it only covers his feet, and he basically gets to lord over all the worms and crabs and tadpoles and his happiness is pretty damn near complete. He invites this turtle to come in and look around and see for himself, and so the turtle does, and after the turtle gets stuck in the mud, he climbs right back up out of that well and starts telling the frog about the East Sea where he comes from. He tells this frog that even a distance of a thousand miles can't give him an idea of the sea's width, and even a height of a thousand feet can't give him an idea of its depth, and he tells this frog that in the time of the Xia dynasty, there were floods nine years out of ten, but the waters in the sea didn't increase one bit, and he tells this frog that in the time of the Shang dynasty, there were droughts seven years out of eight, but the waters in the sea didn't decrease one bit then, either. He tells this frog that the sea doesn't change with the passage of time, and that its level doesn't rise or fall according to the amount of rain that comes, and that the greatest happiness couldn't be to live in a small and shallow well but could only be to live in the East Sea, and after hearing that the frog suddenly comes to realize his own insignificance and becomes very ill at ease and is anything but happy anymore. I can't remember if that's really a story some old man told me on my way to Chongqing or if that's something I heard elsewhere or something I made up or some mixture of those, but it doesn't really matter. Whenever I wake up from that dream, I always feel all right somehow. It doesn't matter where I am or what I'm doing. I just somehow feel okay.

After Ynez found me lying in that alley, she took me to a friend of hers named Milko who was a porter at the Somerset. Milko had two years of medical school back in Bulgaria where he was from, and he helped fix me up. Among other things, I had three broken ribs and a lacerated spleen. I also had an epidural hemorrhage and a skull fracture. He told me I was lucky Ynez *found me when she did and said if I hadn't gotten medical attention then, I wouldn't have made it through the night.*

After a few weeks, we left Chongqing. I don't know if anyone was looking for me, but I wasn't about to find out. Ynez heard about some opportunities in Chengdu, so we went there. The city was growing faster than Chongqing and we both found work at a factory that made tablet computers and we even managed to get a small place. A year after we got there, Ynez got pregnant, but it didn't take. The next winter, she got pregnant again, and in the summer, you came. We called you Meifeng, which means beautiful wind. Don't get too fond of it, though— the name you know me by isn't the name I was born with, and you might find yourself needing to change your name at some point, too. It's sometimes better just to stay unattached to things.

You weren't but a few weeks old when the factory cut wages in half because of all the Kurds who were coming in and willing to work cheap, so we made our way south to Guiyang, where a lot of companies were moving their green energy plants. That's where I started writing these notes to you. I've got no property other than what we've got with us, and I've got no country or roots anymore, but I've got some hard-earned experiences I think will help you. I think they're more valuable than money or property, anyway, if you can use them and avoid some of the things I haven't.

After Guiyang, we headed even farther south toward Colombo Port City in New China, where we got work at a solar panel factory. I took a second job nights as dishwasher, and for a while, things were good, and your mother was finally studying again, which she'd all but given up. You were learning Chinese even faster than me, but then the cell phone companies started slowing down because no one was using cell phones anymore. Then the technology companies that replaced them started moving their factories to Africa because it was even cheaper there, and I lost my job and couldn't find anything other than work at the refineries, which was dangerous and didn't pay that much. Then we heard about some opportunities in Ürümqi, so we packed our things and moved on again. The work here's steady and it pays all right, and the city's growing even faster than Chengdu and Colombo Port City, but I've been hearing even more and more about Lagos and Kinshasa and about all the opportunities there. We're already looking into it, your mother and me.

Our plan is to just keep following the work.

ACKNOWLEDGEMENTS

I wish to thank Luke Gerwe, Anne McPeak, and Ryan Quinn for their editorial guidance.

Thanks also to Kathryn Davidson, Rob Tregenza, Piotr Mikucki, Andrzej Mellin, Ellis Freeman, and Darrell Fusaro.

Last, but not least, I also wish to thank my family.

ABOUT THE AUTHOR

Kirk Kjeldsen received an MFA from the University of Southern California and is an assistant professor in the cinema program at Virginia Commonwealth University's School of the Arts. He also regularly teaches at the Deutsche Film- und Fernsehakademie Berlin (dffb) and the Polish National Film School in Łódź. He is the author of the novels *Tomorrow City*, *Land of Hidden Fires*, and *The Depths*, and he wrote and produced the feature film, *Gavagai*. He lives in Germany with his wife and children.

CPSIA information can be obtained
at www.ICGtesting.com
Printed in the USA
LVHW030326210519
618456LV00005B/578/P

9 780998 465753